MURDER U. A. V.

A CHARLIE KOMENSKY MYSTERY
BY CHARLES A. TUREK

ALSO BY CHARLES A. TUREK

CHARLIE KOMENSKY SERIES

TIMEMAPPER SERIES

NOVELS

NON-FICTION

Charles A. Turek

MURDER U.A.V.

A Charlie Komensky Novel

Pagination Books, Albuquerque, NM, U.S.A.

This novel is a work of fiction. All characters, people, places, events, and organizations are a product of the author's imagination. Any similarity to real people, places, events or organizations is strictly coincidental, with the exception of background historical facts.

ISBN-13: 978-0692295779
ISBN-10: 0692295771

Murder U. A. V. *

*Unmanned Aerial Vehicle

A Charlie Komensky Crime Novel

There was no way that Marco Cajo could have known the chillingly close proximity of Death. Although there are many men and women who go through life with a heightened awareness of their mortality, even of the need to live life to the fullest before it comes to an unexpected end, I couldn't tell you if Dr. Marco Cajo, PhD, was one of them. Hell, I couldn't even tell you what living life to the fullest would be like.

My name is Charlie Komensky. The Charlie is a nickname for Charles, and my middle name is Joseph, after my father. I'm a private detective. If you've read the books and stories about my other cases, then you know that I'm usually not the one who tells the story. I know some book pushers from an old case from my dark ages, and they told me I could get a better deal from a movie producer if I dispensed with the middle man. Said there was a market for something called a first person. So I decided to give it a shot, even though I ain't the first person to try.

Living life to the fullest probably isn't on my resume; I just live it from day to day and try to keep one step ahead. I'm no saint, but I know right from wrong, and I don't tolerate wrong very well. When I screw up, it's usually big, but not criminal. When criminals screw up, I'm here to catch 'em . . . or kill 'em.

But back to Death and Dr. Cajo. Hey, maybe that would be a good name for the case. Anyway, I pretty much know where Dr. Cajo was just before his untimely demise. They found his fancy-schmancy BMW parked in the southwest lot of the museum complex after the incident, and the motor was still warm. That was about 2:00 a.m. on that April night. By "they," I mean the CPD, Chicago's Finest. My contact there is Chief Terwig. He's not a chief of police, and his name isn't Terwig, but you'll get the gist as the story moves along.

If Cajo lingered at all on his way into the museum, it was to enjoy the exceptional solitude of a cold Sunday night in early spring afforded by the grounds between the museum and the football stadium. By first accounts, Dr. Cajo came from a slum in Venezuela. Something called Petare; makes the worst Chicago neighborhood look like Beverly Hills. Some say it even makes Hell look appealing. Depending on who tells it, his family had six or eight brothers and two sisters plus Mom and Dad living in a shanty the size of a garden shed. Calm came only on the rare times the whole family fell asleep. Quiet was when it got so cold out that none of the half million people in the slum wanted to be out in the streets fighting or killing each other. Solitude didn't exist. To be trite but honest, life was as cheap as a lawyer buying lunch. Cajo managed to pull himself out of the slum, get an education, and nail a sweet job at the museum. At least that was the back story. When I first heard about him, I thought he did it by his own grit and willpower; but I had a lot to learn about Dr. Cajo.

During my "beat cop" days on CPD, I often experienced the solitude of McFetridge Drive myself.

McFetridge, the namesake, was a labor union guy and did some other things for the city that made them feel guilty enough to give a street his moniker. Not too guilty, because it's one of the shortest. It runs east and west between the museum and the stadium. The landscaping is superb in any season; for me, any landscaping that's not just grass is pretty damn good. In the middle of a dark, moonless night, the two buildings seal off a lot of sound, the lake to the east is a silent mass of nothing, and the high-rises to the west, beyond the Illinois Central tracks, are randomly lit pillars of steel and concrete that amplify the lake's nothingness and throw it back at you. If the night is cold and windless, the traffic sounds from Lake Shore Drive evaporate into the sky like fog lifting off a cornfield.

(For those of you quick to jump, I'm a railroad nut, so I know there's no Illinois Central anymore. Those tracks will always be IC in my mind.)

So there stood Cajo, contemplating whatever brought him to the museum at two in the morning, and, at least in my detective's imagination, enjoying the solitude of his last minutes. If you went on social networking—I call it Face Crap—you could find photos of Cajo that showed him to be a tall, thin man and elegant dresser. That night, he had put on a long overcoat with suede inserts and an oversize collar that offered an extra windbreak. He was dark complected with straight, jet black hair, but his features were European; no native Venezuelan blood despite his poor beginnings. On the other hand, a dentist could have used his smile for a "before" ad, and a plastic surgeon could have had a big payoff with the gross scar that started under his right nostril and ended under the jawline.

The museum had a policy of allowing its researchers to come and go as they pleased and to conduct their studies at any hours. Dr. Cajo had been with the museum for just under three years, so he wouldn't have had to spend much time showing his ID badge to the lonely rent-a-cop stationed at the only door to the museum that could be used for entry at that hour. The trouble is, he didn't. He didn't spend any time at all. To hear the rent-a-cop tell it next day, Cajo just broke from whatever solitude he was experiencing, suddenly ran north up the steps, burst through the door, passed the startled cop, and ran through the metal detector that lit up like an alien spaceship in a 1970s sci-fi movie.

Wide marble stairways flanked the south entryway where Cajo entered, and beyond it, on his left, a staff-only elevator operated by a key card provided access to the research suites up in the lofts above the second floor exhibit halls. Back when the museum was built, architects were all-out gangbusters for the Grecian temple thing. I think I'm supposed to call it Neoclassical. The windows for the research suites were hidden in the square decorations that the designers thought would adequately substitute for Greek friezes. I don't think they had anyone who wanted to spend that much time chiseling naked Greeks into the side of a building, and silly putty hadn't been invented yet. So the windows were right up under the eaves about as high as you could go on the side of the building.

According to the surprised door cop, nobody was chasing the agitated researcher, but Cajo acted like a combination of the Four Horsemen and the IRS was on his tail and took off up the stairs before the guard realized that Cajo didn't sign in.

These days, unless they are off-duty law enforcement, mall cops, bank cops, museum cops and big-box store security have about as much authority to think outside the box as a congressional staffer. If they carry guns, which Door Cop did, their bosses don't want the guns used. Door Cop, whose name was Eddie Figg, found himself in a gigantic pickle. He didn't know whether to let it slide, a serious breach like not signing in looming large in his inexperienced mind, or whether to go after the running researcher; so he did the next best thing and made a cell call to his supervisor.

The call still rang on speaker when Figg heard the sound of voices yelling from upstairs. He pocketed his iPhone without ending the call and started up two steps at a time after Cajo. It was later estimated by those who do that kind of crap for a living that the super picked up the call before the out of breath Figg got to the top landing. The super, whose name escapes me but I'll think of it, later reported that he said hello three times, and all he heard was the sound of dress shoes on stairs followed by Figg calling out Dr. Cajo's name, he guessed from the top landing. Then he heard running, thought he'd been butt dialed, and cut off the call.

The way I saw it, Figg didn't get an answer, so he went running in the direction of Cajo's lab. Between the top landing and the lab was a long corridor, narrower than a hall in a budget motel, running east almost half the length of the museum, and then another running north about half that length until you got to the lab. The direction Figg ran, the hall running north had office and lab doors on the right and windows—those Greek windows I mentioned earlier—that look out onto the Drive and toward the high rises across the tracks to the left. Figg's initial statement was that he had just rounded the corner when he caught a flash of light out of the window on his left and then heard the explosion in Cajo's lab.

Let's just say that Cajo's lab was the bridal suite in this bizarre institutional hotel. The museum board must have thought Cajo would be plucking the cherry on one hell of a sexy piece of scientific research in there to give him so much space. The long hall ended at Cajo's doorstep, which was blown away by the explosion, leaving what was left of two workspaces and an ample, oak paneled office with a fancy safe for "preserving specimens." Did I forget to mention that this is a natural history museum? Not your usual place for doing biological research, but more on that later.

Going back to Figg's initial statement, he continued to run toward the explosion even though part of the hallway's west wall made a fish net look solid. When I first read the statement, I didn't think that he suddenly grew a pair, but I couldn't prove otherwise at the time. Figg's testosterone level aside, he unsnapped his holster, drew his piece, a nice little Sig Sauer P220 Carry weapon, and thumbed off the safety. Just then, he says, a black man wearing a tattered sweatshirt, bleeding from the mouth, and waving a gun, blew out of the tattered doorway opening. Figg raised his weapon, allegedly yelled stop or I'll shoot, then pumped two rounds into the man. One of Figg's rounds took off his left ear, and the other perforated his aorta.

Here's where it gets a little dicey. Figg says he was still so concerned about what happened to Dr. Cajo that he plunged headlong into the smoke and fire of the laboratory, only to lose consciousness just long enough for the black guy to bleed out. By the time he dials 911, it's too late, and the first responders are already getting to the scene.

So, at the end of the long night, we've got a white novice cop who can't get his story straight, a Ph.D. researcher dead of explosive trauma, and—as it turned out—an African-American museum janitor dead of one of two gunshot wounds. You wouldn't need a private detective like me to figure out that Figg was going to be charged with a homicide. At least you wouldn't think so. So let me take a step back and tell you how I got involved in this case.

CHAPTER TWO

Initiating sex and not finishing is not a good omen. "Do you want to shower with me?" Linda asked.

Coming from her, this was an unusual request. We'd had our ups and downs, although ours were more like wing walking in a flying circus than the Camp Cartoon kiddie coaster at Six Flags. Linda never initiated sex. On the other hand, maybe she just wanted me to get cleaned up.

Linda Chelwood was my fiancée and lover. We'd been together almost since I left the Berwyn PD and started my own private eye business. She'd accepted my unexpected proposal of marriage over a year before that, right after we both got pretty banged up on a case, and before she realized that I wasn't in a big hurry to set a date. She'd put the brakes on the whole deal a couple of times, only to relent when I did something so sweet that she couldn't resist me anymore. At least that's my story. Hers was that she had to get back with me before I accidentally killed myself, and her in the process. Maybe this was payback. Like the shower scene from psycho—cue screeching strings.

I guess she was right about my likely getting myself killed, though. I got right up from the movie I was watching and followed her down the hall to the master bath as she dropped her robe. She couldn't have done the runway fashion walk better if she'd been wearing eight-inch spikes. It was one of her things. You can imagine me trying to shuck my shoes and Dockers as I tailed her.

After my last case paid off with a big bonus from the diamond cartels, whose property I had recovered, I could have gotten myself a fancy condo near my office in Oak Brook and put my rundown Berwyn bungalow on the market. It was Linda who convinced me to move in with her. I suppose that's some kind of initiation of sex of a sort. Come to think of it, she had actually initiated the whole damn relationship. But I didn't think the living together deal was because I'd moved up financially. I think it was more that she wanted to keep an eye on me and make sure I didn't blow it all on fancy surveillance gear and paying my CIs too much. I have to admit, I was resting on my laurels a bit, just working my auto recovery angle with the insurance companies and not actively seeking high-profile cases. Living in her big bungalow on Riverside Drive and pooling expenses conserved enough cash that I could afford to spring for a craft beer instead of Old Style now and then.

It's a damn good thing that old girlie mag fart had never seen Linda the way I was seeing her at that moment, or she'd have been living in the mansion and posing for every cover. Linda was my age—not old enough to remember both Kennedy assassinations is what I'll admit to—but she had the body of a supermodel and the face of an angel. That day, she sported a new gold stud in her navel that complemented the fact that she was every inch a golden blonde.

I didn't know a whole lot about Linda's past, and I liked it that way. Back when I took the empty co-op office space in Oak Brook for my detective agency, she was already running her card and gift shop in the mall. I assumed she had money or an investor or something. I must have walked past that shop half a hundred times before I saw her closing up one night and she just stepped right out into my path, wearing a pair of skinny jeans and a low cut sweater, and stopped me cold. Not that I'd never had the women throw themselves at me for one reason or another. I'm a reasonably decent looker, or so I'm told, and having the broads offer a nipple shot or a roll in the hay to get what they want is part of being a private dick—no pun intended. As I said, I'm no saint. It hadn't been past me to take a few of those rolls when the opportunity presented itself. But I could see none of those other babes were in, let alone near, Linda's universe.

If you want to say I was smitten, I won't try to argue with you. We talked the rest of the evening, back then, until night security came on shift and threw us out. In the next few months, she helped me get my accounting and financial statements on track, helped me get a small bank loan, and, simply stated, became the operations manager of my agency. We were business acquaintances, then became friends, then a couple, and then lovers. She never spoke of her family, and I never asked. I knew only that she'd once been involved in a relationship, or a marriage, that ended in disaster. It couldn't have been her fault. She was to me the sweetest and most patient and tolerant person on the face of the planet.

But back to the shower. On that day, at that moment, I would have instinctively trusted her with my life and with the few secrets I kept. As I stepped in with her, I'm sure she could see I was ready for business. One of the great things about showering with a woman is getting behind her and wrapping her in your arms and feeling all of that soft, soapy flesh rubbing against you. I made sure that she couldn't reach around and try to stroke me so that she would get the pleasure of my hands on her first.   I know it's not the usual measure of compatibility, but we fit together. My left hand fit around her breast, first the right and then the left. My right hand reached between her legs and her lady parts felt right at home. As I pulled her closer to me, my man part fit, too.

Then the damn doorbell rang. Why the hell did she have a doorbell that you could hear in the shower? One day I'm going to find the people that invented doorbells and telephone ringers, then work my way up to alarm clocks, car alarms, and, for good measure, the voices attached to transit cars, elevators, and GPS. You know what I'm going to do to those assholes! Anyway, the mood fractured into a million pieces. Initiating sex and not finishing was not a good omen.

After kissing Linda softly on her neck and reluctantly removing my hands from her naked hips, I found one of the two oversized bath towels she kept next to the shower, wrapped it around me until the Velcro caught, and trooped off to the front of the house. As I passed the guest bedroom, where she kept a modest home office, I glimpsed what appeared to be a uniformed police officer in the gangway just under the window.

In case any of my readers have never seen a Berwyn bungalow, let me just explain the layout of the layout there. Unlike the inventor of the doorbell, the guy that designed the Berwyn bungalow—okay, I'll give you that it maybe should be called a Chicago bungalow—was a genius. Though they came in sizes from the small crap-sized two bedroom, one bath that I owned, to the king four and two with a rental flat in the basement and in-law apartment in the attic dormer—like Linda had—they all had one thing in common: The Dutch basement. This is a foundation basement dug only three to four feet into the ground. Basement windows start with a sill at ground level and may go up to the basement ceiling. Said another way, it's a bottom floor that's half below ground. But the main floor living area in a Berwyn bungalow is always above the basement, elevated four or five feet above grade, and giving a raised and extended view out of the main floor windows.

For a cop, this is tactical dynamite, defensible ground, the equivalent of a small hill or a raised bunker on the battlefield. My first thought after seeing the uniform in the gangway was that Doug Christie, my ex-cop buddy who now freelanced for the DHS, had some deal going and sent a go-for to fetch my help. Just in case I did have to hold the hill, though, I snatched my .38 from its holster slung across the easy chair and tucked it into my Velcro. Its muzzle felt chilling against the naked small of my back.

Before I could get through the living room to the front door, somebody pressed the doorbell twice in quick succession, followed by a hard pounding on Linda's heavy hardwood door. Four bangs, then a husky female voice called, "Department of Homeland Security! Open up!"

"So it's Doug's people," I thought, and relaxed a bit. So as not to expose myself any more than the towel already did, I stood a little behind the door as I clicked off the deadlock.

"Now!" Keying on the click, someone heaved the heavy door inward from outside, threw me off my balance, and literally knocked me on my can. The can and the beer I'd been drinking before the shower squirted out from under my bruised ass. When I looked up, there standing above me were two gargantuan female DHS agents in full body armor and pointing automatics in my disadvantaged direction. Behind them stood a mixture of DHS, FBI, and local police, if I read the Kevlar right. No Doug to be seen.

"Linda Louise Chelwood!" shouted the larger of the two.

"Do I look like a Linda Louise?" I realized that my towel had fallen open a little and there probably would be no dispute, but just then Linda walked in from the hallway. Surprised and wearing the other towel pulled up over her breasts in a terrycloth mini-dress arrangement, hair wrapped in another towel, she quickly tried to hide herself.

The second female agent shifted her aim from me to Linda and yelled, "Don't move. Linda Louise Chelwood. I have a warrant. You are under arrest for terroristic activities and capital murder." Linda's eyes went wide, but before she could say anything the second agent had her roughly handcuffed and proceeded to frisk her in a manner that I thought was unnecessary, given her state of dress. I quickly thought of going for my gun, but just as quickly dismissed that as foolhardy and reckless. This had to be a mistake that would resolve itself. Linda started sobbing.

"You Komensky?" This came from another DHS agent, male, who had stepped behind agent number one while I watched the big bag of DHS dirt molest my fiancée.

"Who's askin'?"

Instead of fighting me on it, the guy turned toward the bunch of cheap seats outside and said, "Christie? You want to get in here and secure the boyfriend?"

Doug emerged from the maddening crowd and offered me a hand up. "You might want to get yourself dressed," he suggested.

"Not until you tell me what's going on." By this time, a uniform had gone into the back and emerged with some clothes for Linda, and the DHS greyback was hustling Linda in the direction of the door. "Hey!" I yelled, still from the floor. "How about some Miranda warning?"

Doug reached down and gripped my right arm hard to catch my attention, and mostly to keep me from doing something I'd be sorry for. "Patriot Act," he stated without emotion. "You know they don't have to."

"Patriot Act sucks."

He lifted me to my feet. "Gun!" yelled the officer with Linda's clothes, but Doug was quick to disarm me and, with a gesture, stop anyone else from laying hold of me.

"As much as the Patriot Act might suck," said Doug as he deftly removed the rounds from my .38 and placed it into the hands of one of the other officers, "these fully patriotic men and women have a warrant and are going to search the house. I'm going to keep an eye on you. This is a favor they did for me, Charlie. If you don't like it, I can let them take you into custody." I started to say something, but he held up a talk-to-the-hand. "Hear me well! You can go with her, but then you'll be in no position to help her."

I muttered something about needing no enemies, and then watched from the front window, still in my beer-soaked towel, as they put Linda into an unmarked DHS utility that bristled with more antennas than an embassy in Pakistan. When the utility pulled away, my heart jumped into my throat, and I stood at the window for another twenty minutes before Doug convinced me to pull on my Dockers and a sweatshirt and sit down.

"You still haven't told me what this is about." I'm sure my irritation showed through. "What the fuck?"

Doug remained stoic. "I just can't, Charlie. If I tell you too much, it'll taint the investigation. You know how that works."

I stood up, incensed. "Taint the . . . Fuck the investigation! That's my girl!" But the uniform positioned in the hallway gave me a dirty look and Doug tugged the sleeve of my sweatshirt. His face said I should shut up. "Do I need a lawyer?"

"They won't let you have one."

He was right about that.

After two hours of watching six DHS evidence techs go through Linda's place like roaches in a pantry, I was still sitting in the easy chair with Doug sitting across from me. He tried to make it look like he was keeping an eye on me, but, knowing Doug, he was probably just asleep with his eyes open. On the other hand, I spent the time making mental notes of what I could see, of where they had been, and of just what items they carried out the front door.

Within the first hour, I know, they took Linda's two computers, both our cell phones, my .38, and a file cabinet, presumably with all the files that were in there when they arrived to serve their warrant—which I never saw, by the way. After that, the items they confiscated were about as random as a drunken hockey match: Two novels and a cookbook, a couple pair of shoes, a bottle of cologne, an empty three-ring binder, bras, panties, two pairs of exercise shorts, everything in the medicine chest including my aftershave, and a makeup case that I know Linda only used when she was on a trip. They must have shot hundreds of digital photos of the house and contents and at least one video. I heard them rummaging in the basement, but anything they found there they must have taken out the back.

Then I thought about our cars. My water damaged Taurus had been broken down in the garage for a couple of months, but Linda's Mercedes had been parked out front. I got up and went to the front window. Her car was gone; I assume confiscated along with the other "evidence."

Like they were responding to Pavlov's bell, two salivating FBI agents in the usual combination of white shirts, dark suits, excessively shined shoes and too little room under their armpits for the holsters came in the front door at exactly four o'clock. I didn't realize one of them was a woman until they motioned Doug out of the way and sat down on the couch with him. She looked particularly capable of snapping all of our necks if need be, but the male agent just looked capable.

"S'matter?" I asked the woman. "Not enough money left in the DHS budget to fritter away on me?"

Doug gave me a look that asked, "Now? Really?"

Never one to know when to leave well enough alone, I added, "Do Penn and Teller know you stole their act?" Doug winced.

The male agent took his time getting out a notepad, while Doug's eyes kept pleading with me not to say anything else. Then the female agent spoke. "I'm agent Barry, and this is agent Pincus."

"And?"

"We don't like two-bit private dicks any more than DHS does," she growled. "It's just that your particular situation seemed to fall more on our side of the fence."

"And what is my particular situation?"

"You are friends with a known member of organized crime." She made it sound like she was talking about belonging to the AARP or Costco, but she had to be referring to Georgio Luchesse. Georgio had been born into the Sicilian mob, but had been working with police as an undercover informant for several years. I had working arrangements with a few other wiseguys, just low level information stuff, so I couldn't be sure.

"Who would that be?" I bluffed.

Agt. Barry chose not to answer and continued, "So an FBI profiler was called in to assure that you answered truthfully under interrogation."

"And that would be you?"

"Yes. So I assume you have no problem with answering a few questions."

"Oh, I don't know. Let me see my calendar. I think I have a dinner engagement."

Doug couldn't hold his water any longer. "Charlie, just answer their fucking questions so we can get out of here."

"Well! Why didn't you say your questions involved fucking? I'd be more than happy to demonstrate." I was sorry I said it the second it came out of my mouth.

The big male agent was on me faster than a cat on a hamster. Before I knew it, he had hooked the links on my handcuffs and pulled my arms up behind me and over the back of the chair. I heard my shoulder joints crack and felt the jolt of pain in my whole rib cage. Doug just watched as Agt. Barry put her shiny-shoed foot into my groin and pressed. "You're the only one getting fucked today, Shithead! Okay, first question: Where were you at 2:00 a.m. night before last?"

"I was right here, masturbating to an episode of Survivor on the TiVo."

Agt. Pincus pulled harder and I thought a shoulder dislocated. "Here. Right here. Watching a DVD."

Pincus relaxed, and I took a deep breath while Barry continued, "What is your relationship with Linda Chelwood?"

"She's my girl. My fiancée."

"That all?"

"We have sex. Would you like a threesome?" Pincus pulled. Now I was sure the shoulder dislocated.

"Does she run your business?"

"Not formally." My sense of humor was getting a little thin, but I added, "Just badly."

"Does Linda Chelwood belong to any radical organizations?"

"None that I know of."

"Does she know Georgio Luchesse or any of his associates?"

"Just since last year."

"Where was Linda Chelwood at 2:00 a.m. night before last?"

The more times I get interrogated by the police, the more I understand what it's like for the real criminals: Always trying to outguess the cop, never knowing if even the most innocent answer is going to get you in trouble. And trouble could be anything from a whack across the shoulder blades from the "bad cop" to five years in Statesville. Trouble for me was I didn't know where Linda had been.

Barry persisted. "Cat got your tongue?"

It was too late for them to not notice my hesitation, so I gave them the only right answer. "I don't know."

"You don't know? Do you want me to believe that?"

Here's the beauty of it. I could take it to a polygraph. "Yeah. That's right," I spit back at her. "After half a bottle of red wine, I sleep pretty sound. So I don't know for sure where anybody was between 10 p.m. when I shut off the news and 7 a.m. when the alarm went off." For good measure, I added, "Do you know where your partner is at every hour of the night?"

I waited for the obvious throwback. The "gimme" that would force me to lie, but it didn't come. Maybe, I thought later, it was because the house on Riverside Drive was so close to the scene of whatever crime this was that Linda got herself involved in, my sleeping hours didn't narrow it down well enough. But I knew that Linda had not been in the house at either of those times. Hell! I guess if I was a better fiancé, I would have asked her the next morning when she wasn't at her gift shop until after 11 a.m.

Barry and Pincus kept up the staring contest, but they flinched first. Pincus let me relax my arms and then, on a nod between him and Barry, took the cuffs off altogether. Now I had at least one bad shoulder to go with my game leg. "He's all yours," Pincus said to Doug, just as I was about to get up. I realized that the rest of the joint team—it was a taskforce, but I abhor that word—had finished executing the search warrant and disappeared. My two interrogators soon followed, leaving the house quiet.

Doug still sat on the couch, looking my way, but not really, like he was taking in everything but avoiding eye contact. "You know what they say about making eye contact," I said, playing on it. I wanted to beat him unconscious, but I knew it wouldn't get me anywhere. "So keeping in mind that I'm just a hair this side of homicidal right now, I think it's time you tell me what's going on."

Sitting at Linda's kitchen table and sucking on Linda's last two beers—bottles of Belgian this time—he talked and I listened. We worked slowly through the details of Dr. Marco Cajo's explosive demise, or as much of the details as Doug could or would tell me. When we were both Chicago cops, I had trusted my life to Doug Christie more than once, the kind of battlefield faith you had to have in your brothers in blue if you were to psychologically survive another workday, or any workday, on the streets. I'd elevated myself by taking the officer's exam and getting put on the waiting list before taking a detective's grade offer from the Berwyn PD. Doug had made lieutenant, but never practiced the healthy skepticism required of the working detective, the skepticism that kept creeping into my dealings with Doug over the past couple of years since he'd become a "contractor" for DHS. Mercenaries, whether they called themselves contractors or whatnot, bothered me. It said that DHS either didn't have the savvy to hire its own good people, or it had some dirty work to do and needed plausible deniability.

"You still haven't told me how Linda's involved," I said. I pointed the beer bottle at Doug as if I were going to poke an eye out with it. "What the hell is she doing in DHS custody?"

He finished the last of his, and winged a left-handed toss that landed the empty in the now overflowing garbage can in the corner. "First, they called me in and wouldn't tell me anything other than it involved you, Charlie," he answered, seeming sincere. "Then I said that I didn't want any part of an operation involving a friend unless I knew enough details. You know? When they finally relented and said it was not you, it was your girlfriend, I said no a second time."

I got up and dropped my bottle gently into the can. "And yet, here you are." I gestured around me to point out the mess made by the search of the kitchen. "Right in the middle of the shit."

He didn't say anything right away, but, as I sat back down, he pulled his chair closer to mine and leaned in. "Charlie, I don't know exactly what they've got on her, but I do know that she's in some deep shit. Like Boston Bomber shit. And I know these hardasses. The ones we were dealing with on the locomotive case are Princess Pussycat by comparison. These fuckers are planning on holding on to Linda for a long, long time. When I heard a couple of 'em talking about there's also a cybercrime involved, I thought maybe they planned on sweeping you both off the grid. Cyber terrorists wind up in a floating prison somewhere near the Solomon Islands. No cellphones, no networks, no satellite connections. Nothing. So I recorded a tape, left a copy with Terwig downtown, and signed on to make sure your asses didn't vaporize like Hoffa."

"You think it's okay to be telling me this now?" I looked around, trying to spot any listening devices that could have been planted.

"Just right now, I don't care. But don't get too wordy just yet."

Doug retrieved a signal meter from his jacket. After taking about ten minutes to sweep the house, he declared that all known DHS and FBI frequencies were cleared. When he put his jacket on to leave, I stood up. "Can you get me in to see her?" I asked.

"Not a chance to slim fucking chance."

"Where are they holding her?"

"It's not in Itasca. That's all I know." Both of us had been in the DHS facility in Itasca, but it stood to reason that there were more. "I think you should call the judge.

CHAPTER THREE

L inda's big house was bigger and emptier without the DVR, the cell phones, and the computers. After I scoured the place for any other drinkable adult beverage, I just sat and let the whole mess sink in. Kind of like cat piss sinks into your living room carpet.

My next reaction was to call the Berwyn PD for a favor, but I decided that I'd burned those bridges and pulled one too many already. Terwig was probably out. If he'd promised Doug not to listen to the recording, he wouldn't compromise that for me.

I wanted to call Judge Elmo Burmeister to help me out about as much as I wanted to call Charles Manson to organize a family picnic. A retired judge, he was another part of my past, another part I found hard to trust. Less than a year before, I found out that Burmeister's judgment had gotten my cop father killed in action while trying to get evidence on the Chicago mob. Before that revelation, Burmeister had been my mentor and replacement father, but the revelation about my father's death came with the admission that he'd been seeing my mother behind Dad's back. It made my trust fall off a wall and never try to get up again. In part, I had the aforementioned small-time mobster Georgio Luchesse to thank for the whole Burmeister debacle.

No calls of any kind were going to get made unless I got my hands on a secure phone. Fortunately, Linda's house wasn't far from my office. DHS already would have tapped my office line—with or without a warrant—but I had a couple of burner phones that I'd kept in my document safe after buying them to stalk a stalker. I'd scared the stalker so badly that he left for Canada as soon as he made bail, but my rich lady client still stiffed me on the expenses. It was either keep the phones or blackmail her into paying my bill with some pics of the stalker watching her and a virile young man who was not her husband do the pokey with his hokey. Seemed like a lot less hassle to just keep the phones. Even if the feds had searched my office, me being the confident bastard that I was, I was sure I could detect whether they had picked the lock on my safe.

I threw on a light jacket to cut the chill of the night and made sure Linda's place would be secure. Hell, I had no idea when either of us would be back there. The spring evening had turned a little windy, and a light overcast obscured what stars you could normally see above the urban lights. Without a phone, I had to walk over to the newspaper stand on 26th and Harlem to have the vendor, an old acquaintance, hail a cab. In times past, the now slowly shrinking ranks of paper hawkers filled the valuable role of eyes and ears on the street for cops and detectives. I still used them when I could, and paid them well for it, so the vendor was glad to do it.

Once in the Discount Taxi—"We take you where you want to go, but we never take you to the cleaners."—I had time to think. I decided I would call Burmeister only if I had to, and that "had to" would be to get into the DHS lockup to see Linda. Otherwise, I was going to get on the blower to Georgio, and let the chips fall where they may. In my last murder case, I'd seen to it that Luchesse's boss went down for a few months on an assault rap, but he had solid connections inside the Chicago PD. This would also bypass Terwig; in his own way loyal, God bless him, even if the tarnish around the edges of his superintendent's badge dulled the gold plate.

My two priorities: Getting Linda out of the hands of DHS and finding out how she got into this jam in the first place.

Quiet ruled after dark in my Oak Brook condo's office-retail complex. My digs sat above a storefront that sold knockoff perfumes and oversize gangsta baseball caps. As sleazy as that sounded, this was Oak Brook. The only floor space in the world with a lower crime rate is inside the Sistine Chapel. The low crime rate made it more likely that the muscular looking guy in jeans and a leather jacket I saw when I got there was DHS or FBI trying to watch my office from the shadows.

As I stepped into the outer office, where a receptionist normally handled me and the six other office tenants, and closed the second level door behind me, I could see muscle man still lurking where I had first spotted him. In my own small office space, the light on the message center speed-flashed like somebody had found a way to inject Red Bull into the system. Of the twenty-three messages, ten were from the same unidentified caller. I imagined some distraught housewife calling because hubby had bolted with the kids or the bank account or her sister, or maybe one of my insurance clients wanting to know, urgently because it couldn't wait until business hours, if I had successfully turned the salvage 2006

Audi into cash for them. But I had to focus. No new business tonight. Linda was my case, even if it had to be pro bono. I had to get Georgio on it as soon as possible.

When I turned on my desk lamp, it lit up only the mess of unfinished work on my desk, so I flicked it off again. Working only with the little bit of light that struggled through the small, back window, I confirmed that the safe hadn't been opened, retrieved the burner phones and activated one of them. The remaining two went into the inside pockets of my jacket. If they had been here, they either hadn't found or didn't care and left my backup Glock 22 in my bottom desk drawer. Thinking of muscle man outside, I made sure I had a full clip and enough ammo and stuck that, too, into my jacket.

In the dark, I settled into my tattered desk chair and put two calls in—one to Georgio's cell and one to his land line at home—leaving a shrill message at the former, followed by a text. Urgent messages to mobsters, to get any attention, had to be the equivalent of a declaration of war on a small country. Georgio owed me nothing, but I owed him. If not for his intervention awhile back, I would have never recovered the suppressed memories that revealed the truth about Judge Burmeister and my father, or the fact that Georgio and I had grown up together. It's a long story you can read in The Steam Locomotive Murders.

"Swell," I thought after trying to call the judge and getting no answer and no message center. "My life's going to shit, and he's probably out on a train trip somewhere."

The footfalls on the balcony outside the receptionist's area startled me before I had a chance to try texting the judge. I drew my .38, leaving the Glock for backup, and listened, carefully limiting my breathing to slow and shallow. Old buildings are like old men: They creak and groan and make snapping noises in the joints and don't do any more than they have to. My office complex had been built out when Oak Brook was just a little burg with nothing but a few overpriced ranch houses, back in the 60s, about when I was born. The good thing was it was before the tree huggers got their hands on the testicles of the nation. No heavy insulation in these offices. At night, you could hear anything in the building that moved.

Taking a position behind my office door, .38 at the ready, I slowly turned the doorknob and pulled the door quietly inward. The dark figure had just opened the outer door and stepped inside. But it wasn't muscle man. This dark figure was definitely female—slim in tight, black workout clothes, full, well rounded breasts, shapely hips followed by a hot caboose, with the hood of the light sweatshirt pulled up over her head to conceal her face. She didn't seem aware of me, and held a small, brown envelope in her left hand.

"Halt!" I issued the command as I swept into the room, .38 aimed for a kill. She issued a little, startled, feminine squeak, the kind that told me she wasn't used to reacting to deadly surprises, and froze. But before I could ask her to put up her hands, the popping of an automatic from outside, and the shattering of my suite's front window, startled us both.

I wouldn't have chosen to run back outside at that moment, but that's what she did. She bolted and ran to the left—as I gauged the shots, she put her back to the shooter. Being the prudent ex-law enforcement that I was, I didn't see the upside in trying to give chase under fire.

Instead, I worked my way up as close to the front door as I could without exposing myself. This didn't give me a one-eighty outside, but enough to see that there was no more muscle man—at least not in his original position—and the gal from my outer office was nowhere. I gave it a few seconds, grabbed a paperclip basket off the receptionist's desk, and squeezed out the front door, low and slow. That didn't stimulate another shot, so I tossed the paperclip basket out onto the walkway; enough noise to supply both range and direction to an experienced shooter. Nothing!

When I looked the other direction, Sweetie in Sweats' absence, and her brown envelope laying on the walkway, were the only things left of the whole incident.

How long do you wait to expose yourself after you've been shot at? For me, it's a count of five banana after not seeing any movement. That's when I picked up the envelope and carried it back into my office. Just for good measure, I checked out the back window, but I didn't think either the slinky delivery girl or the agency shadow were coming back. It made me wonder why the girl was a more important surveillance subject than me.

Okay, so I'm not usually the most patient guy in the tri-state area. But a mystery envelope that may or may not have anything to do with the case—who was I kidding?—seemed like too much for my little baby plate to handle. That's why I tucked it into my jacket, took the keys to the six salvage vehicles that my landlord told me time and time again that I couldn't park in the back lot of the complex, and found one that could still be driven. Ten minutes later, the dust that had accumulated on the sofa in my little bungalow during my stay at Linda's choked me as I tried to call Georgio again. No surprise that I had to leave another message.

At that time of night, my old neighborhood could have been the place where feral cats go to get bored to death, but I felt better there than at Linda's, at least for the short term. I popped on the TV and found the cable still working. Unexpected, because with no use for it after moving in with Linda, I hadn't paid their bill. The local news channel was apparently still all over the explosion at the museum, and the anchorman's yammering gave me a few new ideas. For one, this dead Cajo dude had supposedly developed some pre-historic DNA protocol that bolstered evolutionary theory but upset some of his colleague's ideas about pre-humans. It also upset some religious groups. For some reason, the talking heads on the news always read "religious groups" as synonymous with "nut jobs." As opposed to the "reliable sources," read as "unimpeachable," which had told the media that Cajo had received death threats. But the biggest part of the story for the headline mongers wasn't the religious angle. As always, race beat religion by a wide margin. The media were already speculating that "enhanced" charges would be brought against the security guard who had had the misfortune to pop the janitor, now identified as one Laxalt Johnson.

I woke up the next morning in front of the TV with the weather babe telling me what a beautiful spring day it was going to be. The TV would never have got me awake, but my land line did the job on the third ring, at which time my old-fashioned answering machine picked it up. The voice leaving the message sounded like a cross between Elsa Lanchester and Eartha Kitt—slightly Brit female with a lisp tempered by the lousy speaker.

"Hello, Mr. Komensky. This is Bethany Rodolf-Pea. I'm very disappointed that you haven't returned the many messages that I left at your office late yesterday. You came strongly recommended by our most influential trustee, and the museum board has asked me to retain your services. If you are available, I will be here in my office at the museum all day. However, if I do not hear from you by five today, I will be forced to seek a recommendation for another investigator. Bye, bye, now." The last three words had been breathy, and sexy.

Fortunately, I'd activated the burner phone for data as well as voice. A quick search confirmed my suspicion that Judge Burmeister was, in fact, a trustee of the museum, and that Beth Pea was the general manager, and she was a looker. Her photo on the museum's home page could have been the defining standard for posting a fake photo on a dating website.

I could feel the hand of Georgio in this, making the choice to go to the judge for me. Or maybe it was Doug. Even if I'd remembered the judge's position on the board, I probably wouldn't have called him to solicit work. To get to Linda, yes, but not for work. I didn't have the time or the heart to worry about that just then. Hell, I'd be at the museum before Ms. Pea could have her second cup of mocha java latte if it meant getting Linda out of the hands of Homeland Security.

Not wanting to do anything to hurt my chances, I showered, shaved, put on a white shirt and—ugh—tie of dubious cleanliness; even used cologne. The advertising for the only cologne on my shelf suggested it would make me smell like a masculine flower after spending a week in combat and stopping on the way home to visit a children's hospital and train a German Shepherd to play the piano. As I grabbed my jacket to leave, I felt the brown envelope from last night still stuffed into the pocket.

What could it hurt? I tore it open and found a piece of plain, white paper, the kind you tore off a pad of old-time typing bond from the cheap office store. Carefully written in pencil, in a woman's hand, the words said: *"Hermana Chelwood está en peligro de muerte."*

If I remembered my Spanish-olo correctly, somebody besides me actually gave a shit about Linda—or wanted me to think so. But what was this "sister" crap? *Hermana?* And who? Just one more lead I'd have to follow up on as soon as I could get up to speed.

CHAPTER FOUR

I had to give the weather bimbo credit. She nailed the weather right on the head. Bright sunshine, blue skies, and a light west wind that barely made waves out on Lake Michigan. I've been known to bust into a situation without putting on my thinking cap, so I thought I'd take a few minutes walking around the outside of the museum before I went in and talked to Bethany Pea. That, and I wanted to watch a few commuter trains scurry north and south on the old Illinois Central. A couple of South Shore trains were an added bonus.

A giant orange tarp covered the west end of the third floor and roof of the museum, so the only clues I could see on my walk were pieces of scattered debris, duly roped off with police tape and marked by little flags, and the burned tree branches scorched in the heat of the initial explosion. Made me wonder why anyone up there on the third floor hadn't been burned to a crisp. But I hadn't yet seen the ME's report, or the medical notes on the two survivors. Even so, the tarp disappointed me. I'd have to rely on police or agency photos to know if the progress of the explosive on the outside matched what I hoped to see on the inside.

Never one to miss a train going by, I watched another Illinois Central local moving south, then let my gaze wander to the row of high-rise condos west of the tracks. I hoped the uniforms had done a good canvass of the buildings, what with all of the tenants on the east sides having unobstructed views of the museum. Three buildings in particular must have had at least a hundred potential tenant witnesses. Some of them maybe even had telescopes with cameras on those balconies. I didn't care if they were voyeurs looking at sunbathers or just liked to watch trains, like me; that kind of police work solved cases. But I was resolved to doing the leg work over if the case notes weren't rigorous enough. Whose case notes? That was a good question. I hoped it was CPD, because I'd probably die of old age before DHS let me see any of their investigation. And I would have loved to have seen that investigation "before the criminals think of the crime," as my old captain used to say.

Thinking of all these things as I rounded the southwest corner of the museum, I spotted a familiar figure walking toward me. Georgio Luchesse, all five-eight, two hundred ten pounds of him, always played the part of the consummate Chicago hoodlum—from the fifties. That day, he wore his usual slick leather jacket, brown slacks, and well-shined, brown leather Oxfords. The jacket's leather never seemed to get worn, and I used to think maybe he just had a truckload the same size that he just tossed after two or three months of wear, just to keep everyone guessing. Then again, there was a slight change. Conceding to style, he'd gotten a haircut that left only an eighth inch of fuzz. The twinkle in his brown eyes betrayed his serious-as-an-embolism face and told me he would enjoy the encounter. I noticed a leather notecase under his left arm.

"Brother Luchesse!" I called, holding out for a handshake as we got closer to each other.

"What's with this brother shit?" A smile broke more on the right side of his mouth than on the left. "You're still the same fucked up private dick, and I'm still the wise guy I always been. No brother about it. I can't figure out why I don't just pop you an' drop off your sorry carcass with material service." The reference to the infamous quarry diggers of Chicago hinted why people like Jimmy Hoffa never got found. We embraced and back-slapped until the moment got uncomfortable. Then he almost tossed the notecase at me. "Here's what you need."

I glanced around for anyone watching and then looked inside. About a ream of neat copies of the DHS investigation, CPD notes, and eight-per-page printouts of forensic photos and mug shots—small but useable—looked back. Two USB drives rested in the bottom of the case. Georgio saw me wrinkle a brow and volunteered, "I didn't know if you had access to a computer yet, so I did it bot' ways."

"Where'd you get this?" I was worried, but not very. Over the years, my mob friend had helped out so many judges and cops that he couldn't get convicted of spitting on the mayor. He had that many favors coming to him, and we just kept piling them on. The miracle was the mob still trusted him, too. Some of my so-called colleagues in the PI business doubted his value as a CI, but I trusted him. "You rob a Staples?"

"Yeah," he grunted. "And now I gotta get down to Wrigley an' pick some pockets, jus' so 's I can keep up my skill sets. Ya know?" Georgio reached out with his hammy right hand and grabbed my left bicep. It felt like he clamped a steel shackle around it, but the gesture, and the return of the serious look in his eyes, told me what I needed to know: My friend had read the file and saw nothing but tough going and heartache ahead.

With only a few minutes left before my scheduled appointment with Bethany Pea, I found a bench lost in a couple of bushes and started digging into the files. The trouble with reports from two police agencies and multiple officers within anything less than a week after a major crime is the same as trying to clean bird shit out of a bucket of sand with a tweezers. I got the same basic story that I told at the start of this book, but details got as blurry as wearing the wrong bifocals after a three-day bender. In particular, Eddie Figg, the security guard, was as consistent as horse poop on a parade route. He told an inexperienced DHS interrogator, who didn't question it, that he heard not just one, but several explosions. A veteran Chicago cop—an old buddy from Clearing—had him down to only one explosion, but then got him so flustered that he clammed up and asked for a PD.

That got me digging into the M&E file. Chicago had some pretty clever ex-Army munitions men who could pinpoint the source of an explosion faster than you could find a caraway seed in a slice of Jewish rye. But even their report came back muddled. The kinetic profile of the explosion showed that it centered near a floor safe, but to the south of it. The safe had been breached, but the force vectors were wrong, and there were other anomalies all over the blast map, leading M&E to conclude that there could have been two, three, or even four separate explosives planted in Cajo's office. My gut—even holding an egg muffin that had spent too much time on the steam table—told me that Figg and the ill-fated janitor wouldn't have survived a blast map that looked like that; but both did, or the media wouldn't be crucifying Figg and turning Laxalt Johnson into another sainted victim of white racist America.

Two of the biggest questions I had: Where did Johnson's gun, the one he was waving around, come from, and what was he doing up there supposedly arguing with Dr. Cajo? The investigation answered neither sufficiently. The gun had no serial numbers; for all intents a Saturday night special. As far as the other question, I think investigators were just a little too media-squeamish asking questions about Johnson. It took a lot of verbal acrobatics not to be labeled as racist by a media that would assault any question of Johnson's motivations. It's hard to be even-handed when asking questions that are racially charged. My rule is to ask the questions and take the kick in the gut you deserve if you ask them wrong.

Both DHS and CPD had approached the question of surveillance footage in their own ways. DHS had its high-tech boys hacking into every network on the lakefront, without much success. The brass in charge of the CPD investigation had sent uniforms to cover property owners within three football fields in every direction to see who had cameras. The trouble with that kind of low-tech stuff, for something that occurred at two in the morning, is the same trouble you'd have walking into a dark room full of flashlights pointed at you. As for eyewitnesses to the explosion, it would be weeks before the manpower-strapped department could field enough checkered hats to hit every tenant in those apartments across the tracks. Funny, 'cause just as I was thinking tracks, another commuter train rolled lazily toward Millennium Station with a load of mid-level bankers and wannabe brokers who could no longer afford the parking rates in the Loop.

With my appointment impending, I dug into the folder for some background on the illustrious Beth Pea. Pea had been the museum's GM for five years, and before that a political appointee with Cook County. Nothing to suggest terrorist tendencies or the ability to cook up IEDs. The unfortunate Mr. Johnson had done ten stinking years cleaning the kiddie poop out of the urinals on "school" days, and had achieved the rank of associate head janitor. With a job like that, I would've wanted to get shot.

The folder contained a standard background on Cajo, with about as much detail as I have already explained. I would still have a lot to learn. Then I noticed that DHS had also profiled a young lady named Danita Cambrero, the deceased doctor's personal assistant. Her life story, as picked over by DHS, only went back to her graduation from Universidad Central de Venezuela in 2009 at the age of 19. Before her first semester there, she either didn't exist, or lived completely off the grid. I broke out into a grin to think that this must have frustrated the hell out of DHS, an organization more butt-tight than FBI in the Hoover heydays. The profile came with a pretty good glossy of a daintily boob-tattooed Danita wearing a sexy, low-cut gown at some museum event with the T-Rex in the mezzanine growling behind her left shoulder.

The one page writ of information that the feds used for the warrant on Linda laid out the basics of the case against her. Cajo had received an email from her computer. The email stated that she was the executive officer of a "militant Catholic" organization called Creation Militia and threatened "physical harm" if Dr. Cajo and the museum did not cease efforts to establish a complete historic line of DNA from animals to humans. None of the files contained a copy of the email, and I wondered why, but mostly I wondered why I never knew that Linda was involved in such an organization, let alone a Catholic.

I flipped through a few more pages, spotting nothing else I would need for my meeting, and then stuffed the notes back into the case Georgio had given me. Standing up, I noticed that a couple of yellow school buses placarded for the Catholic schools had pulled up on McFetridge, releasing a gaggle of squawking plaid kids plus half a dozen plainclothes nuns and a priest or two. They had populated most of the walk opposite the entrance to the museum. The whole scene struck me as just too weirdly coincidental. One priest stood aloof from the rest. Wearing a black overcoat that was just a bit too warm looking for the day, and a conservative but stylish hat, clean shaven except for a perhaps too venal mustache, he seemed uninterested in the kids, maybe lost in thought, almost meditating. Seemed like too much "too" to me.

I'm no expert on priests. I'm a should've-been Catholic who usually gives them a wide berth, but like a sudden firestorm here Linda got arrested for making terror threats on behalf of some kind of church organization and this place was turning into a church circus. But the longer I studied the priest, the more my gut told me he wasn't with the schools and I should check him out.

No sooner had I put my feet in gear than who should ooze out of the crowd other than the FBI's finest, Agent Barry, sharpened canines and all. Even though I quickly pivoted towards the front door, I knew she would pounce. "Hold it right there, Komensky." I quickly glanced in the direction of mustache priest, but he was gone, and I was trapped.

Putting on my best dog-kennel smile, I turned to the agent, who either hadn't changed clothes since Linda's arrest or, like Georgio, had a closet full of the same outfit with days of the month embroidered on the waistbands and collars. "Agent Burial! What a surprise," I spewed and held the notecase close under my left arm.

"You know very well it's Agent Barry," she corrected as she approached like a storm trooper in a Nazi parade. "You're not supposed to be within two counties of here." Her steel eyes fixed on the notecase. "What you got there, Charlie?" If she caught me with copies of the official investigation, heads would roll and I would be sharing a waterboard with some of Bin Laden's closest confidants.

I still thank God, and perhaps the Archdiocese of Chicago Schools, for what happened next: Before Barry could get her bony fingers on the notecase, a beautiful and seductive blonde woman in her mid-forties peeled herself off from the group and walked our way. The seductress wore a form-fitting black business skirt with a high waist and a wide, brown belt under a sleeveless white blouse, and she had been talking with the nuns. Enough buttons were open on the blouse to call attention to her figure, and she flipped her long hair convincingly to one side as she offered me her right hand. "Mr. Komensky! Charlie!" She purred this so sensually you would have thought we were practicing lovers. "Thank you for retrieving my notecase for me." Instead of going for the handshake, she picked it from under my arm; I didn't resist. In one continuous move, she secured the notecase under her left arm and, to my surprise, embraced me in a way that startled and aroused me. To this day, I'm not sure that she didn't put her tongue in my ear as her cheek brushed mine.

Without allowing a second for either of us to think about it, she turned to Agent Barry, whose standard-issue, man-in-black suit wilted by comparison. "Agent Barry," she exclaimed as if they were old friends. "I do hope the FBI is doing everything it can to keep these innocent young school children safe." I could see Barry's eyes getting agitated, like lotto balls on drawing night, and I don't think she expected what happened next. I sure didn't.

This time the embrace, way beyond what some would consider appropriate, took a few seconds longer. With Barry standing a head shorter than the blonde temptress, I'm sure she got a shot of the breastworks that any red-blooded guy could only dream of. Then the woman kissed Barry full on the mouth—not a long kiss, but not a peck either. I couldn't help but put my right hand over my mouth to keep myself from uttering something profane.

Before I knew it, the blonde had taken my arm and started ushering me toward the museum entrance, leaving Agent Barry dumbfounded and stewing in her own juices; pun intended. "I don't make assumptions in my business," I said as we walked. "But I'm going to assume you're Beth Pea."

Looking straight ahead and smiling as though what had just happened was everyday business protocol, she said, "In the flesh." She held my arm in a way that crackled with sexual electricity and made the word flesh seem that much more naughty. "I knew you from the picture on your Internet site," she said confidently. "Which doesn't do you justice, by the way."

"Well, thanks for the save."

"I assumed that you might have some information that you didn't want to share with the feds, that's all." She giggled just a little. "That sexless little so-called profiler is easy to rattle."

By this time, we'd reached the security position, the same one where our erstwhile guard Figg had presided over the incident. Seeing Pea, the current guard waved us through. Though I expected to be escorted to the third floor, Beth Pea instead took me to her sumptuously paneled executive suite on the second floor just above where we'd just come in. I noticed that her windows gave her a beautiful view of the football stadium and the park in between, and that Agent Barry was no longer standing out on the walk dripping juices. I'd forgotten about the priest with the mustache, but he would resurface much later.

As she offered me a seat, quite a comfortable one, I might add, Ms. Pea said, "Did you know that FBI agent interrogated me yesterday for four hours?" I said I didn't. "And she had the gall to ask me if I'm gay."

"Are you?" The question seemed appropriate, given the scene she had just made outside.

She sat down behind her almost empty desk. "It's just because Dr. Cajo's assistant was my roommate for a time when she first came to town." Her eyes met mine and held them, inviting me to continue the line of questioning.

"You didn't answer my question."

"Let's just say I'm a free agent and leave it at that, shall we?" A sly smile crossed her lips, then vanished. "Now, how can I help you help the museum?"

"Just where did you and Cambrero . . . I mean, where were you roommates?" I guess my mind was making the same connections as Agt. Barry, and I hoped there was a cure for that.

She squinted at me, and then almost winked. "Now you're interrogating me."

"Shouldn't I?"

"My flat is right over there in the high rise." She pointed, not out the window but at the west wall of her office, on which was hung a rather cheap looking print of a prehistoric cave painting—of lions, I think. "If you are outside," she added, "and you know where to look, you can see my balcony."

I filed that away in my gray matter and decided we needed to stop beating around the bush. "You can help by telling me your take on what happened."

"Obviously," she began, "somebody wanted to hurt the museum. Dr. Cajo was as important to the museum as a decent quarterback would be to the Bears, or a decent coach, for that matter."

"So it's all about the museum? You don't buy the theory that this Creation Militia was behind it?"

She took a deep breath and thought a few seconds. "Listen, Charlie. May I call you Charlie? I know your fiancée is in jail over this. I know you want to get her out. I just don't have anything concrete; it's a visceral feeling that there's more to this than a cabal of religious nuts bent out of shape over the theory of evolution. After all, the Scopes trial was years ago."

"And yet, that cave art is what? Ten thousand years old? And we've still got artists who can't draw a better lion than that. Is that a lion? It's a lion, isn't it?" I hated to play devil's advocate against Linda, but I needed to see if the Pea gut was shakable.

"And we've still got people who believe that humans came from ancient astronauts, so I guess creationists aren't all that extraordinary. Still. . ." Her thought trailed off.

"You know something about Cajo that might not be in these files," I said as a statement, not as a question. If you accuse a witness of something vague, nine times out of then they'll spill something new.

"Marco Cajo came to us with impeccable credentials," she started again. "But the circumstances were still unusual. Museums don't usually hire strong research academics. It was almost like the old days I've read about, where back in the 1920s and 30s an institution would grant a curatorship to any adventurer who promised to discover an Egyptian tomb. We had a position open in South American antiquities, and Dr. Cajo insisted that it was the perfect place for him to showcase the rewards of an expedition he had planned, an archeological expedition back to his home country of Venezuela. I'm not sure why us. I'm not even sure why Chicago, except that he'd already been an adjunct professor at UIC for seven years. He said he'd already approached all the other colleges with an anthropology department, U of C, Northwestern, Loyola, Lake Forest, and so on. He said that all of them were interested, but it would take too long for him to achieve the notoriety that these discoveries deserved. Especially since he had a graduate assistant who had developed a computer progression that could fill in the DNA blanks, could prove that evolution really worked.

"I think his exact words were, 'To hell with higher education. We can bring this discovery to the common man.' That rang true with the board, which had, just the year before, approved a new 'all-access' mission statement on the belief that local colleges only served the rich or those with an IQ high enough to get a scholarship—or low enough to be sports jocks."

That made me chuckle, and I observed, "They are academically *verklempt?*"

Beth Pea looked at me slyly. "I didn't know you were Jewish."

"Neither did my mother; that's why I'm baptized." When I saw the look of shock on her face—she apparently didn't have the twisted humor thing going—I added, "I knew this Yiddish jeweler. He's away for a few years for . . . irregularities." I watched her swing her chair around toward the window, so she wouldn't have to look at me. It was good that I had repulsed her to the extent that she would be off guard. "Let's get back to Cajo, sweetheart. Did he get everything he wanted from you?"

"He and I didn't sleep together, if that's what you mean." She continued to face the window. "But if you mean by way of employment with the museum, it didn't hurt that he offered to fund the proposed expedition out of his own pocket. He brought Miss Cambrero and his graduate assistant with him, both of whom signed on for less than some of our let's say 'more mature' staff, but the grad assistant quit before he ever got started. He never filled out any HR forms, and I don't recall his name right now."

I filed that away for future investigation, but I didn't want to lose Beth's story in my questions. "Why don't you tell me what happened after Dr. Cajo got rolling on this expedition of his?"

She flung the chair back to face me like artillery targeting an enemy plane, and her cheeks were flushed and hot as the gun barrels. Something about the conversation, something more than just my bad Yiddish jokes, bothered the hell out of her. "To tell you the truth, Charlie, it was a flash in the pan. Marco was down and back in six months, supposedly with the artifacts, all sealed and approved by the Venezuelans. You know how that goes; with the South Americans, you don't know if you're looking at an official stamp from antiquities or a liquor license. I never saw the artifacts, and neither have any of the children of Chicago or their mid-level IQs. They were in the safe in his office, and now they're not. If they haven't been blown to shit, or stolen by your girlfriend's god freaks, it's your job to recover them."

Pea leaned forward with her mouth opening and closing like she wanted to say something more personal, and then she pushed back and flushed some more.

"And if you want to know anything more about the project or the graduate student, you'll have to ask Danita." She picked up her cellphone and started entering a text as she stood up. "I'll order her to come down and pick you up out on the main floor."

CHAPTER FIVE

I've been given the bum's rush in better ways and by sexier women, but to say that Beth Pea blew hot and cold would be like saying Kilauea and the South Pole were close in temperature. Cooling my heels sitting on a bench in the museum's main hall between a large meteorite and the skeletons of two prehistoric pigs, I reflected that, since flaunting her sexuality didn't bother her, her abrupt end to the interview had to be something else. It seemed odd that she had never seen Cajo's artifacts, so maybe that was it.

Given the size of the museum hall, the amount of limestone in the walls, and the interference of a thousand flashing displays designed to catch the attention of those aforementioned, mid-level IQs, it surprised me that I was getting a good cellphone signal; so I used the down time to leave a few messages and—ugh!—texts for Georgio and Doug. Not, "when can I visit Linda?" but more like, "what have you done to get me in to see Linda, and if not, why not?"

As I was just about to call Chief Terwig, Cambrero walked over. I recognized her from the DHS workup, but those pictures didn't do her justice even if the casual clothes she wore most certainly did. A white Oxford style shirt, open to the third button, and a pair of the kind of skinny jeans that appear to have no actual seams, or sewing, graced a slim figure that kept some meat on the bones where all the meat belonged. Her long hair, black as a flush in clubs, fell easily into the open shirt and competed with equally black, full brows and dark eyes. The entire package approached on a pair of spike heels that put her just a peel over my height as I stood up to greet her. Something about her walk reminded me of Linda; but then, Linda never left my mind.

She stuck out a hand to me in the way that younger women do when forced to shake hands, as if bending the wrist down might possibly make you decide not to participate. "I've been ordered to meet you down here," she said, suggesting boredom. I've seen material witnesses try to put off their interrogators with the same attitude.

To disturb her as much as possible, I shook her hand vigorously and, since I left my notecase on the bench, even placed my left hand over the clasp. "Charlie Komensky, Miss Cambrero. My condolences for the loss of your . . ."

"Yeah, just say boss and get it over with. I already told the other cops that I only slept with him once." She managed to wriggle out of the handshake. Almost as if she had memorized it, she added, "And Dr. Cajo was a great, honorable man who I respected very much for making me realize that we had both made a mistake. So as not to poison our professional relationship, it was never to be a topic of conversation between us."

"Did your boss have any enemies?"

Something flashed through those dark eyes, but it didn't ignite. "As I said, he was respected and honorable. He was a devout Catholic. I think any man who puts too much store in religion has God as an enemy. I think it colored everything he did."

"You don't like religion much?"

"Not when rational people let it consume them." Again it sounded memorized, as if she repeated the phrase to conceal something she didn't want to discuss. Then she went on, "As a public figure, I'm sure he had his rivals. Even I have rivals, Mr. Komensky. You know how rivals can be. They nip at your heels like nattering dogs. But for rivals, I think, the joy is in taking you down and frustrating your endeavors, not in bringing an end to you in a spectacular explosion." Again that flash in her eyes.

"Who are your rivals, Miss Cambrero?"

"Pardon me, but I don't see where that has anything to do with this."

"Maybe one of them was gunning for you, hoping you'd be in Cajo's office." Then I added, "Where were you exactly?"

"I was home, in my apartment across the way."

"Can anyone verify that?"

"I have this particular masseur named Frederick who was in the process of making me delightfully . . . relaxed . . . when the explosion lit up the night sky. I'm sure he'd be happy to do me another favor and vouch for me."

I must have looked surprised. "No, I don't still live with Beth Pea," she added. "As soon as I was able to get a lakeside apartment in the same building, I moved out."

"So you saw the explosion?" I'd never before had a murder case where two possible suspects lived in a direct line of sight from the scene. "Can you describe it?"

I could see the effort to avoid saying too much change her expression from enigmatic to concerned. "I saw the light. My drapes were closed. When Fred saw the light I got up and looked out. By then, it was all a big cloud of smoke with flames dying back. You couldn't see anything." Then her face went back to playful. "Did you think I would get a naked massage with the drapes open?" Actually, I did, but I didn't say it. Instead, I just asked her for Fred's information and asked if she could take me on a tour of what was left of Dr. Cajo's suite.

On the way, I tried to imagine what Dr. Cajo and Eddie Figg might have seen, and what each was thinking as they ran up the flights of wide stairway, past Beth Pea's office, and emerging onto the third floor. I tried to feel the panic in Cajo's mind. About what? I tried to hear what Figg heard, following, never quite catching up with Cajo until he heard and felt the explosion. How deeply into his suite had Cajo gone before that? Had he spoken to the janitor? What was in Figg's mind when he saw poor Laxalt staggering out of the smoke? Did he see only the gun first, or did he see a crazy black janitor who may have just caused a major explosion? We passed the heavy red stain, the life that had pumped out of the janitor and onto the floor. How long had the guard really hesitated before calling for help?

"So, we're here. What now?" Cambrero's query jerked me back into the present, and I found myself standing at a yellow police tape. The hardwood floor beyond the tape had literally fallen off the side of the building and left a ledge of floor about two feet wide hanging on splintery timber between a wall on my right and the void on my left. Daylight poked through the orange protecting tarp and made the area suggest the innards of a pumpkin being prepared for Halloween carving.

"So you and Dr. Cajo were about to process these artifacts and prove to the world that man evolved from monkey. Am I right?"

She scowled and stuck out her lower lip. "Crude, but rudimentarily right."

"Whoa! Let's hold off on the big words, Little Princess. I'm just a detective. So how far along were you?"

"Again, I fail to see . . . "

"Just humor me."

She sighed. "In all fairness, we were nowhere. Marco didn't show them to me when he got back from Venezuela. Once he locked them in that big safe of his, it was like he was waiting for some kind of sign from God. I suppose that's unfair, since he had to reconstruct Code Pimp's work."

"Whose, exactly?"

A wicked smile lit up her dark features; she gave me just part of the answer to let me know that she wasn't going to make it easy for me. "That's what we all called Marco's graduate assistant."

"I'll ignore that you're having too much fun evading. So did Pimp have a Christian name? Or any kind of name that would be recognized by any religion?"

I stand by the general idea that liars always talk too much, and experienced liars talk more than novice liars. If Danita Cambrero's explanation of why she didn't know Code Pimp's real name had been any longer, we could have submitted it for a *New York Times* article. It amounted to this: Even at UIC, Cajo kept his anthropology work separated from his biochemistry work, so she had never met Code Pimp face to face. I decided to let it go, assuming there were records at UIC that could be mined.

"So show me this safe," I ordered more than asked. The files said the safe was largely intact, though opened by the explosion, and that concerned me. I never saw a floor safe that couldn't withstand a heavy impact, a major fire, or an external explosion of any kind unless the door of the safe had already been compromised. I had a case once where the burglars dropped a six-by safe off the roof of a four-story building, and it didn't bust open. But take a half-inch diamond drill to the right spot on the door and a few ounces of RDX triggered from the outside, and the safe will spring open like the trunk of a '56 Buick.

Danita said, "I'm not walking across that broken flooring." She backed away a few feet to show that she meant it. "The safe is on your right after you pass that broken partition. You can't miss it." A snarky wish for good luck went unspoken. "Plus, you're a cop and you can go past the tape and I can't."

Another general truth I go by is that there's not a woman alive who can't get out of something by pretending to be squeamish. To argue would be futile, so I asked, "Will you just stay put until I get in there? I'll holler back out if I have any questions."

She didn't answer, but stayed put, so I started across the abyss. It actually wasn't so bad; just had to watch out for a spot where the old subfloor had splintered. The structure creaked and groaned, but seemed stable enough, and there was enough width to let me keep my balance, even holding the notecase Georgio had given me. Once I reached the breach in the partition, the floor ahead seemed more solid, as if the explosion in that portion of the building, at least, had been concentrated upward rather than directly out the side. Around the shattered partition, now, and out of sight of Danita Cambrero, I pretty much had the scene to myself.

Out of respect for the lowly CSIs who toiled under some of the most gruesome circumstances, I used the hand condoms I had brought along to poke and lift and move anything that appeared of interest. You never knew when this or that police detective would need something new from a scene this fresh; and, as it was, whether Cambrero knew it or not, I was not supposed to be inside that yellow tape. To summarize the scene as a chaotic mess would be to minimize the damage done by the blast. A 500-piece jigsaw puzzle made from a chaotic mess would be solvable. One made from a picture of Cajo's office would not be.

Whether by chance or intentionally—maybe Cajo was carrying the bomb—the explosive had done a number on the anthropologist, as evidenced by the multiple remains markers for large body parts, and the numerous markers for minor remains, significant only from a ballistic spec's point of view. Beyond that, the "windshield bugsplat" patterns that hadn't been destroyed by heat said that a credible portion of old Doc Cajo was still in there with me.

From what I could make of it, the room had been Dr. Cajo's main work and study area, housing three desks and rows of now-destroyed bookshelves against three walls. What books hadn't been blown out into the night as confetti were shredded, scattered and charred by the blast heat. Even so, the investigators had clearly marked areas where they had found and taken as evidence those books or subjects that might give them insights into the workings of Cajo's mind.

Had they taken any reading material from Cajo's residence? I would have to take a closer look at the contents of the files, which I had placed on the remains of a desktop.

A blown open door in the partition opposite where I had come in lead to a smaller office with two desks, and to a closet and a room with a sink, shower and toilet. The heat char extended through all, even though it appeared to me that these inner rooms had sustained no other significant damage, and that the desks were unoccupied before the fact. A marker in the bathroom suggested that the authorities had confiscated Cajo's cursory toilette as evidence.

Cajo's floor safe stood like the big, hulking shell of a blown out bunker in the northwest corner of the main office. The big gold leaf letters signifying the manufacturer declared its strength, but the heavy door, at least five inches thick and hanging from one hinge, declared its surrender. The side that nominally faced the hallway where Cambrero waited showed blast marks as deep as any I had ever seen on a safe or vault door. That could explain the broken hinge, but nothing could explain the door bolts pulled in and the lock handle pointing down, the almost universal position of an open safe. That wasn't in the notes. Had the detectives missed it?

Inside the safe, again, I found just soot and char. The old safe was just one massive open space inside; no shelves or drawers, not even the indication that something had been stored in boxes. Grabbing the police file, I looked for the pages about the safe. No. None of the investigators had logged any safe contents, meaning they were gone when the scene was sealed. Everyone had just assumed that the explosion blew the safe when the hinge failed, and left it at that. It seemed to me that the artifacts were key to motive, though I realized that the authorities already thought they had motive. This—the safe being open—changed things. Yes, an explosion this hot and powerful could have destroyed the artifacts that were going to make Cajo's career and the museum's reputation; if they were in the explosion. If they weren't, then where were they?

The burner phone squawked a dissonant squawk, drawing me away from the inside of the safe. The text that appeared came from Doug Christie, down there on the bottom with God and Jesus on the list of people I expected to hear from after the night before. Batman was higher. The text said: **L xfer ext so museum 10 min. L wants to talk to U.**

They were transferring Linda from holding to God knows where, and they would pass by in front of the museum south entrance in ten minutes so we could talk! I had to get down there. "Danita!" I yelled. I had so many questions I needed to ask Linda. "Danita, I'm coming out!" No answer came back to me, but I wasn't going to let that stop me.

Before last year, I would have told you that I didn't feel guilty about anything. Guilt is for suckers who think that God is going to give them a do-over; the guiltier you feel the closer you are to redemption. So I shoved any feelings of guilt aside. Screwed up my relationship? She just wasn't the "right one." Shot the wrong suspect? Not my fault he was in the wrong place at the right time; besides, he needed shooting. Never visited my mother? She had her life and I had mine. The Berwyn Police psychiatrist once told me that there was a fine line between reasonable denial and criminal psychosis. The bad guys didn't feel guilt, either.

Then Georgio Luchesse opened my eyes to a real psychosis; I'd gone so far to suppress or excuse guilt for my father's death that I repressed important memories. After that, not only did I question every decision I'd ever made, every alliance I'd ever formed, every friendship, every battle, every move; but worse, I couldn't tell if trust was real. Did I get trust because I was worthy, or was I buying it? Did I give trust based on facts, or only on facts that I chose to remember? And the worst part? I felt guilty that I had no answers to these questions.

Linda had said the introspection made me a better lover and friend. As teetering on the edge as our relationship had been before my epiphany, she stayed with me, so I guessed I must have been. It didn't make me a better detective—that's for damn sure. In Charlie's Official Book of Detective Work, the gut ruled and the head and heart were only along to see that the gut didn't take a .45 slug before solving the case.

There on the verge of the broken floor outside Cajo's onetime office, I could see myself in line for fifty minutes with a shrink. Bad enough thinking of myself in the third person, but guilt over Linda and guilt over possibly missing this chance to hear her side of the story had me in a panic. Now, nobody panics in a vacuum. You either panic because you don't know enough about what is going on around you, or because you know exactly what is going on around you. The former seemed to me the probable cause in this case, confirmed when I realized I hadn't noticed how the wind had picked up outside the museum. The big, orange tarp, formerly held by its weight fairly closely to the contours of the damaged building now flapped and bucked like a mainsail in a thunderstorm.

I stepped out onto that unstable shelf of damaged floor and got whacked in the side of the head by a giant wave of orange that knocked the notecase out of my left hand and sent me tumbling into the abyss of splinters, broken steel, and abrasive granite rubble. I felt a sharp pain in my right side and came to a stop dangling from a giant broken timber whose sharp, splintered end had pierced my jacket and hooked into it. Blood poured from a gash somewhere under my right arm, and I couldn't find a handhold anywhere. I took a deep breath to yell for help, but the pain put my lights out like a power failure in a coal mine.

CHAPTER SIX

Getting knocked out is God's way of telling you your head's not made of iron and also telling you who's in charge of when you wake up, if ever. There's not a whole lot you can do when you're unconscious, unless you look at missing things as doing something. In my case, I missed two important funerals.

Dr. Marco Cajo's was the first funeral. I would have liked to be there to question whoever showed up, whether the feds and CPD liked it or not. It's always the unexpected visitors to a memorial service that have something to hide. Murderers, it seems, like to make sure their victims are really dead; that the giant hole in the back of a skull or the knife sticking out of a gurgling chest wound wasn't just a figment of the imagination—unless it was.

But I was confined to a hospital bed with machines beeping out my respiration and tubes sticking into embarrassing places. I suppose no real harm was done to the investigation, even while the harm that my severe head injury may be doing to my brain was being debated by my doctors over morning Starbucks and the printouts of my bodily functions on their iPads. I eventually would learn that CPD had done a thorough job of staking out the funeral.

Probably the most remarkable thing about it was the glaring absence from the funeral of any of Dr. Cajo's immediate family. As I recalled, in my stupor of waking after three weeks up on the grease rack, Cajo had a mother and two siblings, both of whom he had gone to great lengths to bring to the United States after emigrating himself. None showed at the funeral; not by itself a damning fact, but something to be suspicious of. CPD had been judicious in taking photos of every visitor, analyzing the handwriting samples photographed from the bereavement book, and determining the identity of anyone who failed to sign, or just watched things from the sidelines. All the players I knew so far were there, and plenty more from the museum and from Cajo's tenure at UIC, among them about two hundred former students. None were flagged as bearing any recently exercised grudges. Nothing suspicious about the attendance at all three days of the wake by both Beth Pea and Danita Cambrero. Absent from the list was the security guard, who found himself in the county lockup on an old misdemeanor warrant while the prosecutor decided whether to charge him with a "hate" crime.

A disturbing part of the whole mess was that the funeral parlor, a respected venue supposedly above reproach, received conflicting orders as to whether the body was to be cremated or buried. It appeared that only upon the intervention of a priest, Fr. Isaac Liebowitz, did the funeral home relent and schedule a proper burial at Mount Carmel Cemetery. Now that was suspicious on its face.

Also in the category of remarkable things that happen while you're unconscious; Doug Christie is the one who was there when I woke up to hand me the police file. "Here's something to take your mind off your injuries," he said as he tossed it onto the bed.

I laughed groggily, then said, "My mind hasn't really been on anything for three weeks, according to the doctor."

It was then that Doug told me that Beth Pea had actually spent more time at my bedside than Doug, and that she had wanted to be there when I woke up. "A pre-scheduled fundraiser kept her," he said.

"Yeah, I know." I did, really. I had seen them before on cases. The kind of fundraiser where you could insult a donor by wearing the wrong brand of contact lens. I've said before I had a lot to learn, but boy did I have a lot to learn about Beth's fundraisers.

"And Georgio," he added. "That wise guy really cares about you."

I admitted it was good to have friends, then started paging through the police file and ignoring Doug's efforts to look solicitous. "Where's the file I had with me when I fell?" I asked. The notion that it had gotten into the wrong hands suddenly hit me.

Doug then admitted that he knew Georgio had obtained the file through questionable channels and that he had let it slide. The file would be in my office when I got back there, and the feds would be none the wiser. "I want you to know how sorry I am about being so hardnosed, and about Linda and all."

This wasn't Doug. Doug was a good guy, but he rarely apologized. At that moment, he looked so hangdog that you could have made dead rhubarb look perkier. "What about Linda?"

Remember I said two funerals?

The news of Linda's death hit me like a line drive to the gonads followed by a two-by-four across the shoulder blades and a bus running over both legs. All my moorings came loose; I mean really came loose. Before I knew it, they were calling the puke patrol and hustling Doug out of the room until they could be sure I hadn't had a brain hemorrhage or something. Two brain scans, a dozen EKGs, three bedpans and enough needles to supply a Chicago street gang proved I had only been agitated by the "news." News? Hell! The crime rate was news. The mayor punching an alderman was news. Troops invading Poland would be news. This was a fucking unmitigated disaster!

When they wheeled me back to the room, Doug sat glumly looking out the window at the sun falling behind the tall buildings of the Near North area. Between the drugs and a small spark telling me I couldn't lose it again, I thought I could handle whatever Doug still wanted to say. I'd been a cop, but I'd never lost a suspect in custody . . . ever. The drugs pushed my emotions—my anger—down so that the worst of it was on the bottom. I'm ashamed to admit it, but on the top sat my cop's distaste for the big no-no of having a suspect die while in your custody; pushed somewhere down on the bottom, and gasping for air, struggled my love for Linda and the grief I thought I'd spend years dealing with.

Fifteen minutes of silence, during which I noticed that Beth Pea had showed up outside the room and thought better about disturbing us, separated me from the truth I so much needed to hear but didn't want to. Finally, I asked, "How?"

Doug kept it short—a rote recitation of the facts. I'll keep it brief here, because it's still painful to think about. Doug plead my case when he learned that DOJ ordered Linda to be moved to a more secure location, whatever that means. That's when he called me; when I was teetering precariously on the edge of the broken flooring up on the third floor of the museum. To accommodate a brief meeting between me and Linda, they'd taken a transport and a regular, federal issue SUV. The transport held a dozen detainees. Four, including Linda, would go to a max-hold in Indiana. Eight would be moved to Texas for deportation after that stop. They allowed Linda to ride in the SUV until our meeting.

When I didn't show up in front of the museum on time, Doug's superior ordered Linda to be put with the five on the passenger side of the transport. Handcuffs and leg irons kept them in their seats. After departure, five real-time cameras on the transport transmitted pictures from the inside and all four directions outside to DHS headquarters. The right side camera showed how a city dump truck ran a red light and tore through the side of the transport, crushing the six passengers on that side. The inside camera confirmed the carnage after the transport rolled twice and landed on the driver's side in a city park. Linda and two of the Indiana detainees died. Everybody else suffered injuries ranging from broken bones to just bruises. The city truck driver fled on foot and had not been found. Simple as that. Doug asked me if I wanted to view the footage when I got out, but I declined.

While I was unconscious, according to Doug, the feds released Linda's body for a small, closed-casket memorial and burial at Queen of Heaven Cemetery. Nobody of consequence came to the memorial: Linda's three employees at the card shop, her accountant, and, surprisingly, Beth Pea and Danita Cambrero. Doug and his wife attended, as did my friend Georgio. Notably absent was the ex-husband. "What was his name again?"

My toasted brain could do nothing for me. "I can't tell you, Doug," I explained. "She only mentioned him once or twice in the last few years."

Like a dog with a chew toy, Doug wanted to keep rolling it over and slobbering on it. "It just seems suspicious. That's all. Like she wanted to keep it a secret."

Some of that anger kicked my drugs in the butt and jumped all over that. "Why doesn't your boss just order the nurse to let me O.D. on this shit? When I get to wherever Linda is, I'll ask her about it!"

"You're not . . ?" Doug looked surprised.

"Suicidal? No, but I'm pretty much going to be homicidal if you don't get the hell out of my room and leave me alone!"

Doug left with his tail between his legs. I knew he'd tried to do me a favor, and it had come back to cause him grief. I had no doubt he'd be on the carpet for the loss of three lives and a transport, but I didn't really care at that moment.

I eased my sore side back into the bed. Taking hold again, the drugs gave me the ease to run the facts through my mind without getting agitated, but not the clarity to put enough of the puzzle together. I still went on the assumption that Linda couldn't have been responsible for the explosion. Her death? I heard the heart monitor start to accelerate as I thought about it. Her death could have been a true accident . . . or? There was no way I could get my hands on the Spanish note, the warning that Sister Chelwood was somehow in danger of death. I was afraid that anyone I trusted to go retrieve it would turn it over to the authorities out of context, or wind up as dead as Linda.

Nothing made sense. I had one victim murdered by explosive device, a second victim shot to death in the supposed panic caused by the explosion, and now a third possibly killed to silence her. Possibly a fourth and fifth with no clear connection. I had to remember to ask Doug or Georgio to get background on the other two deceased detainees, and why Linda rated incarceration with the group. Maybe I could call Judge Burmeister in the morning and see what he could do to find out who was driving the city dump truck.

More facts ran through the fog in my head, now as thick as the clam chowder at Shaw's Crab House. Facts like uncertain artifacts, unseen by anyone except my first victim and whoever had accompanied him to Venezuela, had been vaporized or stolen depending on how you interpreted the open bolt on Cajo's safe. Two people who had potential ringside seats for the explosion seemed to have alibis. The connection between Cajo and the Priest with the Jewish name—Liebowitz—had to be investigated, along with Linda's connections to church organizations. No matter. Enough diocesan priests ministered to the mob that Georgio could easily do that for me.

The prospect of dealing with a bereaved fiancé must have been too much for Beth Pea. The afternoon of muddy thoughts, bustling nurses, blood draws, and bathroom stops—did doctors even exist anymore?—wore on without her appearance. With the evening meal that tasted and smelled like every other evening hospital meal in every other hospital on every planet in the universe, came a fat Pakistani nurse with a thick accent who pulled my IV, gave me a couple of pills, and told me to behave myself so that the doctor could release me in the morning. I thought of giving her some cash to go find me a cheeseburger or a pizza slice, but I concluded that she would have consumed them or shared them with an equally fat boyfriend, who didn't love her but stayed with her because she always had food, before she got back up to my floor.

Visiting hours came and went. Realizing I needed to adapt my still-clearing head to the passage of three weeks without a conscious version of Charlie Komensky stalking the streets of Chicago, I watched about an hour and a half of cable news—as much as I could stomach of the liberal leftist crap—and then gravitated to the chair to watch the lights come on in Chicago. The orderly that reached in to dim the room light, not noticing that I was not in my bed, did me the favor of making the view of Near North that much more vivid.

I paid no attention to the passage of time. That kind of thing usually happened to me when I immersed myself in a case, but that night it worked in the opposite direction. The changing vistas of the city, the traffic ebb and flow, the patterns of change of neon signs at street level, the pulse of warning lights and patterns of light and dark windows on the taller buildings, and the random surges of pedestrians being squirted across the intersections as traffic gave way all served to hypnotize me, to remove my thoughts to a place where I no longer tried to solve a case; where, in fact, nothing needed to be solved. Though I sat for hours, time either stopped or became of no importance to me.

When traffic in Chicago diminishes to almost nothing, it's usually sometime after all the bars are closed and before the gyms open up—unless it's Sunday morning. Then it's before the churches open up. That's how long I sat looking out that window, and that's when I became aware that Beth Pea was in my room. I couldn't tell you what day of the week it was, let along what day of the month; but I can tell you that Beth Pea was Saturday night beautiful. She stood just inside the door, with the light in the hall outside backlighting her.

Looking back, I guessed she had been at one of her fundraisers. She wore a stunning gown or dress. At the time, at least, it stunned me, and at the same time recalled something from my past; as if it were the first dress that I had ever thought of removing from the woman wearing it.

You'll excuse me if I can't tell you all the details of the rest of that night; partly because of the state I was in, and partly because a gentleman doesn't kiss and tell, at least not graphically. She tried to offer some condolence, some words I can't exactly recall. She seemed duly ashamed that she had been standoffish at the first meeting that now seemed to be years in the past. She halfheartedly tried to stress that I needed to get back on the case. As she did so, I got up and walked back to the bed, where I sat on the side closest to the window. She moved from the door and sat on the other side, she touched my hand, we leaned in and kissed. No time was lost as we helped each other open the backs of our respective garments. Who knew it would be that good in a hospital bed?

CHAPTER SEVEN

That was the second time I slept with a client. Someday, I'll tell you the story of the first time, but not now. So, to make a long story short, I was faithful to my dead fiancée for three weeks, and unconscious for most of that time. Not a five-star review of my will power, or of my ethics.

After getting released the next day, I didn't give it much thought. Beth had already gone when I woke up to the sound of a young nurse filling out my discharge papers on an iPad, the schoolgirl in her alternately giggling and shaking her head like she'd never seen such goings on in a hospital bed. As soon as I had duly signed away my firstborn and agreed to donate six of seven vital organs in lieu of a cash payment of the bill—they didn't want the brain—I hightailed it back to my office in Oak Brook. It would be still more time before I could tolerate the thought of being without Linda at her place or at mine.

It turned out that it had been a Sunday morning, or at least that's what it said on the newspaper I saw in the vendor box on the corner. The rest of the week didn't give me much time to fret about what had happened, either. On Monday, the word that the authorities had taken Linda's case off the priority list hit me like a swerving bread truck on a narrow sidewalk. It meant they wouldn't expend much manpower trying to prove either guilt or innocence, instead concentrating on leads to the bomb builder and any other conspirators. If Linda's name were to be cleared, I would have to do it. Or had I already abdicated that duty by sleeping with Beth Pea?

On Tuesday, Georgio brought me the news that they'd arrested the general manager of the Creation Militia, a 50-year-old male named Alan Horvatnic. "But they let him go," Georgio pointed out. "That'a been me, they'da at least kep' me 48 hours." He handed me a copy of the interrogation transcript.

"Did you read it?" I didn't have much stomach for going through all the background questions.

"Yeah." He thought awhile. "He claimed Linda was a wild card, a rogue operative trying to give the organization a bad name. They didn' want to hurt anyone, just make sure the public, an' school kids in particular, got the truth an' not some mumbo-jumbo DNA bull crap. This Horvatnic guy was a real saint; gave the cops everything they wanted: membership rolls, access to computers, email, everything. I get the feelin' he was hopin' it would nail your girl.

"According to the saint, Linda was never an officer of the group, just a volunteer recommended by some priest. The name's in there somewhere." He pointed to the transcript in my hands.

"Did they find the computer they allege Linda used?" I still needed to mentally hold onto Linda's innocence.

"Word on the street is that the militia HQ was a complete bust. No evidence one way or the other. A few sketchy members, but no connections to bombs or terrorism."

"What about the priest?"

"No word. You know how it is. Everybody clams up when they think they might be callin' hellfire down on themselves." Georgio shrugged and cocked his head to the side as if to say he didn't care about hellfire one way or the other.

But I had a thought. "The priest's name wouldn't have been Liebowitz, would it?"

"Yeah! That's it! I remember thinking his family must have converted or something. But how'd you know?"

"Same priest was instrumental in convincing the authorities to turn our dead anthropologist into worm food rather than make an ash out of him." I chuckled, but Georgio didn't get the joke. "You still got that contact over at Holy Name?"

Georgio crossed himself and replied, "Still hears my confession every Saturday."

"Tell your father confessor we need to know where Liebowitz is hiding himself these days. And tell him that no cops need to know the same information. And, while you're at it, have him say a prayer for Linda."

"Aw! I'm sorry, I didn' even ask. You doin' okay?"

I shrugged and said, "Will be as soon as I can get to the bottom of this."

Georgio's unspoken concern was palpable. If I wasn't dealing with Linda's death, it might have occurred to me to deal with the reasons he had become a reliable friend, but I couldn't right then. It was like before you deal with the dog that's biting your leg, you have to deal with the Peterbilt that's about to run you over. I had stored up a big crate of delayed emotional reactions over the years, and one or two more piled on top before I nailed the top back on wasn't going to change anything.

"You're the detective," he stated. It was his way of trying to get me to say thank you for his help, and I never did. He just stared off into space for a bit, and then asked, "Anything else?"

"Please see what you can find out about a search of Cajo's home." I stressed the please. "I don't recall anything in the police notes I have."

He smiled. "I already done that. A little B an' a little E an' we got what I like to call the open door policy."

"Don't keep me in suspense."

"Ain't no suspense. Ain't no nothin'. His house was clean. Like really clean. No furniture. Just a couple suits in the closet an' some stuff in the bathroom. Like he was ready to leave town on a moment's notice. I'd say he had something big going down and was ready to skip town."

"I'd say you're right."

On Wednesday, after my second night of sleeping on the worn leather couch in my office, I decided to take some air and walk the mall before the noon lunch crowd got there and the smell of tarry coffee, fancy flatbread, lo-cal dressing, and cheap chipotle chicken made me puke. The dream I had about Linda early that morning made me depressed and angry the minute I woke up, and the walk didn't help.

On the way out, I circled around; but on the way back, I decided to take a now-or-never route past Linda's Cards and Gifts, only to find her three employees—two college students and a retired lady—putting up a sign in the window. Not a memorial, it said:

LINDA'S CARDS IS NOW

THREE SURVIVORS GIFTS AND GAMES

UNDER NEW MANAGEMENT

Only a fatal stroke would have kept me from noticing through the shop window that they had already taken out two sets of card racks and put in Nintendo and a table full of comic books.

"What the hell!" I said under my breath.

Then I felt someone tap me on the shoulder. I swiveled to my right and said it aloud. "What the hell!" In front of me stood the overdressed Spencer Dinelli, Linda's accountant—formerly—and my occasional rival for her affections. Spencer stood a half a head taller than me, but I wouldn't give you a piece of chewed gum for his self-defense capability. I didn't trust him, and, right then, I very much wanted and needed to knock him on his ass.

"Glad I caught you, Komensky," he said with a smile as fake as his hairline.

Knowing that a public assault wouldn't help me clear Linda, I swallowed the crap but couldn't keep the threatening tone out of my voice. "You claimed you loved Linda! How can you let this shit happen?"

He held up his right hand in a stopping gesture. "Whoa, there, Komensky! It's in the will. And this is just business."

"What do you mean business? What will?"

I won't bore you with the details, like Dinelli did with me, but let's just say I knew he was a woodwork crawler, and his actions confirmed it. He also confirmed I had a lot to learn about the woman who would have been my wife.

Dinelli knew that Linda had filed a will with a lawyer; and, of course, he knew who that lawyer was. Instead of doing some mourning, Dinelli took the news of Linda's arrest and subsequent death as a business opportunity. He and the lawyer fit together like Goldfinger and Oddjob. Stroke of luck: The will named Dinelli as executor. The lawyer went to court and convinced a judge that the card shop was an LLC not exposed to any restitution order that could result from Linda's conviction. What I didn't know was that Linda willed her stake in the shop to her employees. As soon as a death certificate was issued, the shop went to them, along with a hefty "investment" for "renovations" on the part of the two Bond villains. Though she'd willed the house and two bank accounts to me, they were traded to the judge and would remain "frozen assets" until evidence for or against Linda showed up.

I didn't ask whether Linda left anything to her ex; I just stormed the hell out of there. I made a stop at the mall pub, flirted with the barmaid to get her to sell me a whole bottle of bourbon, and asked her to put my .38 in her safe 'til the next day. She'd done it before, and knew not to give it back to me if I wasn't sober.

Thursday? Well, Thursday was only half a day. After that bender, I didn't wake up until almost two in the afternoon with a racket from the mailman shoving some overdue bills under the door of the office. I'd solved the case twice in my restless dreams, and woke up with the gut feeling that the unidentified graduate student, the one that disappeared after Dr. Cajo moved to the museum, had a lot to do with the big picture. Well, maybe he did; but—like all restless dreams—

they didn't tell me what. Was the grad student with Cajo when they dug up the missing artifacts?

DHS had the connections to tap intelligence contacts both in and out of the country, so I called Doug. He picked up on the first ring. "Christie."

I preferred not answering the obligatory questions about how I was handling things, so I started right off. "I got two bones to pick with you, buddy."

"Hey, Charles! How you doin'"

"Well, I'd be better if you'd keep me in the loop. An' don't tell me you don't know what I'm talking about."

I could almost hear him trying to manufacture an excuse. "You been under the weather for a couple weeks."

"What's the connection between the VIC's empty apartment and his missing grad student?" The question came to me almost as I asked it.

"We're looking into it."

"Dammit, Doug! You and I have been together long enough so we both know you must have a few ideas."

"Okay, don't pop an artery. As far as we know the student left the country right after Cajo decided to go to work at the museum." I heard a long sigh. "And neighbors tell me that Cajo had his furniture moved out just about the same time. Seems like there might be a connection."

"So it's possible the student was in Venezuela when Cajo was digging up his future fame and fortune?"

"Yeah. Possible, but we've got a long way to go to find the evidence."

"Did you check the neighbors? Cajo's neighbors?" I shouldn't have had to ask.

"Cajo still showed up there every night. According to them it was for only a couple hours, and then he'd go back out."

That behavior could be either the habits of a workaholic, or those of a man actually sleeping elsewhere. It bothered me that the case was just short of a month old and there were no real leads. Out of frustration, I said, "I suppose we've got zilch from canvassing the high rises across the tracks."

He paused for a long time, then answered, "You suppose right."

I lost it. "That's bull!" I yelled into the phone. "Even with a brain injury, I know at least one resident who saw the explosion!" It was a slight distortion of the truth, but I didn't care. A month was a long time for a murder investigation to drag on without something tantalizing to grab onto, and I knew the internal workings of law enforcement better than anyone. If another interesting case came along, this one would get about as much attention as a bible in a strip club. When he didn't respond, I said. "I'm going to go over there and talk to every resident that was home that night. I hope that no agents or uniforms try to stop me."

It's been my experience that you don't really have to have blackmail material if you're blackmailing someone who already feels guilty. All you got to do is make it sound like you mean business. I hated to do it to Doug, but he proved that at least somebody over at DHS had something to feel guilty about when he said, "I'll tell everyone to leave you alone, Charlie."

Canvassing a fifty-two apartment high rise by yourself is like trying to roll a football—an American football and not one of those frou-frou damn soccer balls—fifty yards into a cardboard box with one hand. You have to keep a constant eye on where you're going, but you're still going to have a lot of diversions and the occasional backtrack. If you find twenty people who even remember the "date in question," you'll be blessed with extraordinary luck. You can't just ask somebody if they saw anything on such and such a date and take no for the final answer. You have to have an arsenal of questions varied enough to spark a recollection, even if it's only about the night the subject saw Mrs. Smith running down the hall wearing only a bra. It's a start. It gets them thinking.

I thought that five o'clock would have been the cleverest time to begin. It gave me time to retrieve my .38 and still get down there. I could work until Midnight and probably catch every tenant after work, or after cocktails, or after getting home from sex with the mistress. About eleven, I started to think about throwing my canvassing theories off the roof. I'd been on every floor of the building three times, spoken to every condo owner, renter, their spouses, and their poodles—which, by the way, aren't dogs but space aliens who suck energy from people by licking their hands or other parts, and who hypnotize their owners into looking and dressing exactly like them. Of the twenty or so people who remembered the day in question, only three thought they had seen the explosion but then decided that they only saw the news coverage of the damage to the museum . . . terrible thing, etc.

Back on the eighth floor, just about to knock on the door of Apartment 82 for the fourth time, the elevator pinged and off came a lanky man-boy in his late 20s wearing bike pants and a cutoff sweatshirt that announced he was gay as his dog. Literally, the logo said, "Gay as My Dog." The dog—a poodle, of course—looked embarrassed to be on his puce leash with this guy, but dutifully started licking my hand as I introduced myself and learned that man-boy was the owner of Apartment 82, one Marvin Semolino. When I pulled my loose hand up to avoid more dog saliva, the little beast just nosed up under my pants cuff and started in on my right ankle.

"So you're named after pasta?" I asked, being unable to resist the jibe.

"It's a good Eye-talian name," he replied, hands all flappy. "Now what may I do for you, Detective?"

"Were you in your apartment on the night of April 15?"

"Sadly, yes. I was getting over a breakup and consoling myself with a large bottle of Chianti and a few magazines." He keyed a combination into the lock to 82 and opened the door. "Won't you come in, Detective Charlie?"

"Detective will do, thanks." I followed Semolino into a spacious apartment tastefully decorated in greys and black with the occasional pink and red for accents. In front of me, a large room with a fireplace to my left held a large leather sofa positioned to address both the hearth and the view out the large patio doors directly across from me. A half partition on my right opened into another living area with a large TV and an impressive sound system. Off my right shoulder, a well-organized kitchen told me Marvin could cook. I assumed that the bedroom or rooms and bath were off the hall that went off the TV room to my right.

"You look like a beer man, Detective. May I offer you one?"

"I ain't stayin' long." I walked over to the patio doors and slid one open. As expected, Marvin had a great view of the museum. He also had a great view of the Illinois Central tracks. (Again I request: Don't write me; I know it's Metra

Electric or whatever—for me, it'll be IC until I kick the bucket.)

It must have bothered Marvin that I lingered looking down on the spottily lit tracks. "So, Detective, you want to know about the explosion?"

"You recall the date?" I asked, turning to face him.

"Because I was just trying out a new lens on my video camera by panning the lights on the lakefront. See, I bought myself a consolation present. I know, I know. That's not a very well-adjusted way to deal with a breakup. Well, then this horrible explosion just lights up my viewfinder. I was worried that it ruined the light sensor. I know you think I'm not well-adjusted, right? A detective knows these things, doesn't he?"

"I'm as well adjusted as the clock on State and Randolph, buddy," I answered, not thinking that a camera was much of a consolation. "So don't ask me for relationship advice. Okay? Did you actually get video of the explosion?"

"It's just one big flare." Marvin looked dejected, like I had just confirmed that he should be more depressed than he looked.

Other than bitching at Doug and his bungling DHS, or at the CPD uniforms who hadn't found out Marvin's possibly important evidence, I was interested in finding out whether this witness video showed Cajo or anyone else who might have been in the vicinity. "Can I see it?"

As a detective, I find cameras to be a useful tool of the profession. For me, they have to be simple to use and hard to make mistakes. I suppose camera nuts view train nuts the same as I view camera nuts. They're frustratingly exact when it comes to the hobby, and Marvin was no exception. I'd have just as soon he stuff a disk or a thumb drive into some hole and play the damn thing, but he had to explain the process every step of the way. I had to admit it was a help that he had a TV the size of my garage door. He started the video with a loud, "Here goes!"

The screen displayed the beginning frame paused with a big triangular "play" arrow in the middle. On the left half of the screen, the museum sat mostly in shadow. On the right half could be seen the south façade and the bright lighting of the steps and the McFetridge Drive turnaround. The bottom of the frame showed the tops of street lighting on Lake Shore Drive. I saw no evidence of anyone standing outside the museum entrance. "Can we play it in slow motion?"

"Sure." The triangle disappeared and the camera immediately started to pan left. In the bottom margin of the screen, I saw the frame count and the time going up. Marvin decided to give a running description. "I used a monopod for this instead of a tripod, so it's a little shaky. You can see there the lighted area north of the museum and LSD coming into view. There's the Roosevelt Road intersection." At this point, the image of the museum was partially off the right side of the big screen. Then the camera started to move right again, and the row of lighted windows that represented the third floor hallway and Dr. Cajo's suite re-entered the frame.

At that point, just under 9 seconds in, a streak of light starting in the lower left corner of the screen and extending in the exact direction of Cajo's suite appeared. In the next few frames, even though Marvin had been moving his camera to the right, the streak moved from the corner of the screen, zeroed in on Cajo's suite, and then disappeared as the blinding flash of the explosion overwhelmed the camera. "That streak!" I exclaimed. "Did you see it before? Stop right there!"

Dumbfounded, Marvin paused the video and answered, "I never played it in slo-mo before. What is it?"

"Unless I miss my guess, it's some kind of ordinance. Can you play it full speed?"

Marvin rewound and played the short video to the point where he'd leaned the camera on the side of his balcony railing and the screen showed the north end of a balcony two floors below him. He stopped the video there. He had been right, you wouldn't notice the streak of light at normal speed.

Concerned with the preservation of evidence, I asked him to make me a copy of the video on a thumb drive and warned him not to do anything with the original recording. "You don't want them coming for you!" I admonished. Giving him my business card, I left hoping he could resist the impulse to put the whole thing on YouTube.

CHAPTER EIGHT

C onvinced that Marvin Semolino's video showed a rocket attack rather than the explosion of a bomb planted in Cajo's suite, I had trouble controlling my imagination. My mind raced with more questions than a Jeopardy contestant, but they all boiled down to three big ones: How do you launch a rocket in the middle of an urban area without being noticed? Where do you find a place to launch it from without leaving evidence of the launch? And who or what kind of person or organization has the means, not to mention the motive, to do it?

Hovering in the hallway outside Apartment 82, I called Doug and left him a message. As a normal part of procedure, I wouldn't have given so much detail over the phone, particularly a cellphone, but as jazzed as I was, I let slip that I had evidence that would change the investigation and exonerate Linda. I didn't say what it was, but the call would still turn out to be a careless move.

Burying my head in the investigation, and now this new evidence, had made me forget my depression but not the fact that Beth Pea also lived in this building, in Apartment 74. I took it as a sign when the elevator stopped at her floor, one below Marvin's, for a resident to get on. Instead of descending to the lobby, I got off and walked to her door. Did I want to share a break in the case with my client, or did I just want to hop into bed with her again? I couldn't deny that last Sunday in the hospital bed still rattled around in my head, so let's just say that I was as professional as possible under the circumstances.

Beth answered my persistent knock barefoot, without makeup, and wearing a light pink nightshirt. She stood with the door open halfway, clearly not sure she wanted to let me in, and said, "Charlie, I didn't expect to see you here."

"I've got some news," I countered. "Can I come in?"

She started walking back into the apartment without opening the door any further. "And I've had a long day," she said in a tone both resigned and suggestive.

I pushed open the door, stepped inside, and closed it behind me. The single reading lamp on the end table next to a large, white leather sofa backlit her shirt enough to tell me she wore nothing else. The apartment layout was much like Marvin's, with the exception that Beth Pea had better taste in decorating. "I'll be brief," I said, apologetically. "Do you have a computer handy?

In the dim light, with the lights of the lakeshore showing through the open balcony door behind her, Beth Pea still looked sensual and alluring, but in a different way. The aggressive beauty who charmed millions out of rich donors at swanky parties had yielded to the neighborhood girl who was sexy simply because she was sexy. But there was more to it than that. She sat on the far end of the sofa, putting her bare feet under her and demurely pulling the long nightshirt between her knees. She gestured at the coffee table, where a laptop computer lay closed, and propped her head with her right elbow on the arm of the sofa. Had the sexual encounter in the hospital been a dream?

I inserted the thumb drive, found the file, and set the video running in slow motion. At the end of the nine seconds, I stopped it and looked at her, expecting the same enthusiasm. But she simply sighed, "I'm tired and I really don't know what to make of your video, Charlie."

"Fair enough." It didn't take a bullet to the head to make me see that this wasn't like Sunday morning. "I'll have to keep in touch." I pulled the thumb drive and started to get up.

"Charlie, wait!" She reached out to me with her left hand. I took it in my right. "Sit! I owe you an explanation."

Going back into Charlie's magic bag of sexual encounters, I'd have to say that, when a girl wants to explain something after having passionate sex with you, she wants to tell you something like you were lousy in bed, or she's pregnant, or she's getting a sex change operation.

So she surprised me when she said, "I want to apologize for taking advantage of you."

"What?" For a genuine reaction from me, this was a doozy. I don't get much more genuine than completely dumbfounded. As far as advantage-taking, I had thought the pleasure was all mine.

"Look, Charlie. I was out of line on Sunday. You've seen how aggressive I am when I'm on the job as Super Beth, the big, sexy girl that brings in all those big, sexy donors. But I'm just little Elizabeth Piotrowski, the kid from North Milwaukee Avenue, and I'm a sex addict." Still dumbfounded, I looked for some way to fill the silence. She saved me from making a damn fool of myself by adding, "I don't treat it. I control it. It serves my chosen profession well. But I'm not proud of it."

I said what I was thinking and was sorry the moment I said it. "The million dollar fuck?"

She sighed again. "I've been called worse. But I wanted you to know you were different."

"Yeah! I don't have the bank account."

"NO! Charlie, you were one of the ones I like. I don't have many, because the way I control it is to do it once and walk away. I don't want anyone I care about to have to put up with my lifestyle. That's why I pushed you out of my office. Charlie, you're different." I could see her getting more agitated, her breasts heaving under the shirt, making interesting little patterns with the nipples. She leaned forward and kissed me hard on the mouth, her tongue trying to dislodge my fillings, then she pulled back. "No! I shouldn't. Charlie, go! Call my office when you have something. It'll be more . . . controlled."

She pulled away and hunched into the corner of the sofa. I've never been one for airing my emotions, but this one had me all over the place. As for lust wiping out cherished memories of Linda, Beth Pea had done that with the bounce of a nipple. I didn't know what I expected when I knocked on her door, but it wasn't this. Having the object of my love—or at least what I knew as love—die on you felt like rejection. Having the object of your lust—the only reasonable facsimile I had for affection at that time—throw you out felt like rejection, too. The only response I could muster was the only one that didn't hurt what was left of my ego. "I'll go, doll. But I want you to know that it takes a lot more than your pathetic tease to hurt Charlie Komensky!"

I got up and headed for the door with my back to her. I didn't plan on turning around to see her reaction, even if she called out to me. She did. "Charlie!" It was more of an alarmed scream than the pleading of a broad that was addicted to booty calls. But we thank God for little favors, and I thank Him that I hesitated and turned my head just enough to see the red laser spot on the door next to me. If I hadn't turned, the small caliber round would have gone through my right lung. Instead it put a neat hole in the hollow-core door.

Dropping to the floor, I rolled toward the small kitchen, then looked up to see that it wasn't Beth who had fired at me. She still sat on the couch looking a little bewildered at what had just happened. "Hey!" I said in a loud whisper. "Get away from the balcony!" The slug didn't come from inside, that I knew, and the open door to the balcony seemed like the only choice. But how? If you took a straight line of sight from the bullet hole through the balcony door, you came up with only air.

The only thing to do was go black. Beth was ahead of me on this and flicking off switches as she came toward me in the kitchen. "What the hell is happening here, Charlie?"

"My guess is somebody isn't happy that we have that video. I'm calling 911." As I said it, I reached for my cell phone.

Beth asked, "How did anyone know?"

As the answer hit me, I dropped the cell phone to the floor. Its screen lit up, and the red laser dot instantly reappeared, this time on the carpet. It started swinging back and forth like a relentless digital force looking for us; whoever controlled this force, this weapon, had discovered what evidence I had through my call to Doug, and the weapon, the laser sight and whatever else, seemed to be tied to my phone.

It had tracked my location through it! Instinctively, I knew that calling 911 was now out of the question, and that we had to stay out of sight of the open balcony door. Maybe make whatever it was come close enough to be identified.

Fortunately, the breakfast island provided some cover, and I hustled Beth behind it and behind me. I drew my .38 from its shoulder holster, though I had no idea how effective it would be against . . . against what?

Seconds dragged like a heavy corpse across mud. Unwavering, the red dot scanned every part of the apartment it could see from the outside. Every fifteen seconds or so my cell would go dark and the dot would stop, only a moment, and the display on my phone would go back on again in some chilling *danse macabre.*

After about ten minutes, I think the dot—or the person controlling it—decided that it had scanned everything it could. The dot disappeared, leaving the apartment pitch dark. I peered over the top of the island, but could see nothing but the distant lakeshore lights. I shushed Beth and started to stand up, hoping to sneak closer to the balcony and look out.

The ringing of my cell startled me and made me dodge back down behind the counters. It rang three times in the stupid ring sound I had chosen for the cheap phone: Bing, bong, bing, bong, bing, bong. Like the sound of a bell on an old European bicycle. As if that weren't bad enough, the phone picked up the call after that, on the speaker, no less, and definitely something I didn't program into the damn thing. A theme from an old, black and white detective movie started playing at full volume. It caught us both by surprise when it stopped in mid-stanza and the voice of a 1930s actor said, "Yeah! We gotta rub the mug out!" The sequence began to repeat, with the lighted screen of the phone keeping time with the eerie music.

A distraction, and a good one! It almost had me. Like a dog responding to a sonic whistle, I snapped my head to the right to look at the balcony. There, over the balcony and now in the full light of the feature lighting on the outside of the building, I could see a six-bladed helicopter drone moving slowly to cross the threshold into the apartment. The thing couldn't have been more than two feet in diameter, and below the undercarriage I could see the muzzle end of a gun of some sort, and the lens of the laser. I didn't see a camera lens, but that didn't mean it wasn't there.

I ducked back down again. We couldn't get to the door to run from where we were, so we would just have to wait. I gestured to Beth to be quiet, but the look in her eyes told me I didn't have to tell her twice.

Continuing the clockwork precision, my phone, laying there on the carpet, suddenly went quiet just as the red laser dot reappeared. This time its pinpoint hit the wall of the kitchen above our heads. It started its determined scan of the kitchen, moving from left to right and then down a step and left to right again. Inch by inch. Seeing no threat, the drone or its operator would move slowly and steadily into the kitchen until it could target Beth and me.

Thinking on your feet is always a part of the job of being a detective, but using your feet can be just as important. I couldn't have that thing getting any further into the apartment. I knew that it somehow linked to the phone, and behind us, just to the right of where the dot scanned the wall, Beth's refrigerator gave me half a chance to get out of this. I thrust my right leg out, hooked the edge of the refrigerator door with my foot, and pulled it open. The appliance light going on in that dark apartment was like a camera flash going off in a dark theatre. I counted on it dazzling the drone, which I now believed was programmed to go after me but may not be piloted, and allowing me enough time for a more dangerous move.

Giving it a count of two, I rolled out onto the carpet, grabbed my phone, and, with a side-wound pitch that I wasn't proud of, I threw the phone out and over the edge of the balcony. As I hoped, the drone did a one-eighty and fled the apartment, following the phone's downward trajectory.

"How did you do that?" asked Beth as she stood up, looking a bit frazzled.

But it wasn't the time for chit-chat. "No time," I answered. "Just close up the balcony and get down to the lobby. Have building security get hold of the authorities, and then stay put until they get here."

Without giving her a chance to ask more questions, I high-tailed it to the stairwell and sprinted down the seven floors. By the time I burst into the lobby, my bad leg screamed in pain. I limped crazily across to the stairs accessing lower-level parking. That's where I realized my second mistake of the night: Parking a salvage vehicle downtown.

The piece-of-shit car, an 80s Ford EXP, a model that looked like its designer used a wrench to squeeze a cheap version of a Mustang onto the frame of an Escort, sat full float in the guest space where I'd left it. Wheels gone, hood up, battery missing, God knew what else. I'd have to deal with that later, because then all I wanted to do was get to the back of the garage and use the exit that would take me out onto the McCormick Place busway. I needed to see if the drone still hovered over my broken cell phone, and the busway was the only place the phone could have landed.

Before I could get there, the third mistake reared its ugly head. Another drone emerged from behind a thick, concrete pillar and blocked the path in front of me. It must have been watching the car, waiting for me. This one was a little bigger than the first, still with six buzzing rotors but with a body that looked about twice as heavy and armored. Below the main body, as before, hung an attachment that had several ports and lenses, each of which could spell trouble if pointed in my direction.

I decided that direction was the better part of valor and changed mine. To hell with whether its partner hovered over my cell phone, to hell even with the cell phone, this pair had me squeezed like a 30-cent lime in a do-it-yourself margarita machine. I headed for the stairs back to the lobby, which I gauged were too narrow for Drone Two to follow. As I dodged between two of the pillars, a sound like a bumble bee on steroids filled the garage. Just behind my right shoulder, an aluminum reserved parking sign clattered to the concrete floor. I glanced back just enough to see that whatever death ray this was had melted off the heads of the two anchor screws like they were wax.

No sooner did I turn back towards the stairway when the lighted lobby sign above the open door exploded in a flash of light, a burst of smoke and a barrage of shattered plastic. That settled it, I had to return fire if I could, and hope that the machine would see a reason to take cover. Without that hope, it seemed only a matter of time before its partner in remote-controlled assault would be on the scene to continue the squeeze play.

Following the sound, I drew my .38, mentally counted to three, jumped out from behind the pillar, fired a round, and took cover again. I knew I wouldn't hit the thing on first try, but I could hear from the sound of the rotors that the drone shifted position a little to my left, actually away from the stairway. How fast could this thing detect my movements and adjust its aim? I guessed I had to find out by experiment.

Blessed with ears keen enough to hear the buzzing of the rotors, but cursed by the fact that sounds bounced off concrete better than off most materials, I judged that the drone had changed position only slightly since I shot at it. While reloading my .38, I started counting a steady beat in my head. One, two, three. I'd have to keep it up to make it to the stairs. Four, five six. On seven, I fired a shot at a trash bin two pillars away from me. Eight, nine, ten. It took a beat and a half for the rotor noise to shift slightly. One, two, three. I fired another shot, but this time obliquely upward against one of the concrete beams that supported the floor above so that the bullet would ricochet. This time, the contraption took almost two beats to adjust. The more noise, the more time it took the drone or the drone operator to process and react.

There were three open spaces between the pillar where I hid and the stairway. I had four rounds left in the cylinder. I could do this.

One, two. On three I ran for the next closer pillar, firing two shots in the direction of the drone's buzz. I crouched down behind it and waited for the bumble bee sound as it shot a laser blast too late to get me. Again the count. Again two rounds and a pause behind the closest pillar.

Needing only to get to the stairs and start up, I took a deep breath and went for it. I reached the bottom step on the count of two but hadn't counted on the stupid thing being closer than a sweaty jockstrap on prickly heat. Two-stepping it up, I didn't get out of its line of fire in time, and wound up catching a laser burn on the right side of my ankle. I gained the top step with a limp and stumbled into the lobby, surprising a few of the residents waiting for their elevator.

I flopped into the nearest of the overstuffed chairs, chairs that nobody ever used unless it was to tie a shoelace or something, and did a damage report. My right pants leg had been burned through, and a nasty burn just above my ankle had already blistered and broken. That drone was using a laser with some hot radiation. Clever! It would do damage but leave no slugs or shell casings to send to the crime labs. The burn felt like somebody holding a propane torch to my leg. Lucky it wasn't my ass.

And I'd have to get up on my feet and move sooner rather than later. The daddy drone couldn't follow me up that open stairway, but Junior from Beth's apartment could. The realization that Beth hadn't come down to the lobby yet hit me, and something like a shiver went up my spine. I'd left calling the cops to someone who had no connections with law enforcement. Unless she could really convince the 911 operator, the call would be handled like any one of a thousand calls demanding immediate response that night. Maybe it was better. At least the target seemed to be me, and I was in the lobby. I couldn't count on the cavalry getting there before Junior had me in its sights—or whatever drones have.

After weighing my options, and standing my ground with only the two bullets left in my pocket wasn't one of them, I thought I might be safe if I could get to a sub-basement, or to the State Street Subway. There had to be some underground level where the signals for the drone's radio controls got too weak to guide it. Getting to the sub-basement of Beth's building would mean going back down to the garage and getting lucky enough to find the door before the drones found me. So the subway it would be, and I could load my last two rounds on the way.

Outside on Prairie Avenue, the weather had taken a turn. The wind from the lake came whistling around the building corners, making debris whirlwinds that skittered across the sidewalk and then died in a little pile of dust and candy wrappers. Sometimes I liked this kind of spring weather, but if the drones were out there waiting, the wind noise would keep me from hearing them unless they fired at me. I pulled up my collar and started limping towards the subway entrance a block away. The burn made it hard to feel my foot and keep from stumbling, and the old leg wound had started to throb again. I felt about as effective as a one-legged horse in a three-legged race.

At the corner just south of the subway entrance, I thought I heard the beelike buzz of Daddy Drone, turned and ducked, stumbled, and landed splayed out face down on the pavement like a pressed duck on a Chinese chopping block. Good luck that the sound was only one of Chicago's ubiquitous defective street lights doing its mating call. A late-night couple in expensive evening clothes strolled by making comments about the drunk on the sidewalk but completely ignoring the bloody gash on my chin. Ah, Chicago!

Getting to my feet, I really did wish for a slug of Bourbon. My leg would bear almost no weight, and I discovered that the swelling from the burn had moved down into the ankle; it would have to be dealt with at some point.

The last half block to the subway seemed like a half mile, the stairs down another half mile. Neither did anything to improve my condition or my mood. Out of breath, I had just gotten to the platform when I heard it. At the top of stairs. Near the entrance. Above the muffled wind, I could finally hear that Junior had been following me the whole time. Going to finish me off in the tunnel. Just like taking out the pesky rodent with a shotgun blast in the mole hole. How deep would I have to go before the drone's controlling signal got lost?

Without hesitating, I jumped off the platform onto the north track. The few people on the platform never noticed, so they wouldn't give me away, and the drone would have to enter the station in the opposite direction before it could survey the area. Even though I was dealing with the unending pain in my legs, I knew I could be gone into the descending tunnel before the drone detected my location.

I wouldn't say that Chicago's transit system is cavalier about the six-hundred volts of direct current that runs the 'L' and subway trains, but they have a funny way of showing it. I hobbled down the tunnel along the side farthest from that exposed, energized third rail. The third rail in the subway isn't something that an average denizen would need to fear. The act of jumping off a platform or finding a set of appropriate stairs, which would indicate some degree of insanity or desire for electrocution on the part of the person who attempted it, might be a cause for concern. On the other hand, out in the neighborhoods where the CTA runs at street level and crosses many of them, and where the average guy could take a shortcut to the local bar by following the tracks, the most the transit agency does is put a sign on the fence that says, "Danger – Keep Off Tracks – High Voltage." Hell, even New York, where there are plenty of third-rail powered trains, covers the damn things with a contrivance that makes it harder to step on the actual rail.

There's an old story about a Chicago drunk who took offense at being refused a free ride on the 'L.' He decided "piss on the transit authority," literally, and walked out onto the tracks. Barely balancing on the running rail, grounding himself, he took good aim at the third rail. When he later told the ER doctor that he had "burning when urinating," it was not a symptom of venereal disease.

I had time to think of all that as I made my painful way further into the tunnel. Having had a short course in tunnel safety when I worked a few subway cases on the CPD, I knew that I would find safety alcoves and a link between the north and south tunnels every two hundred feet or so between stations. So as I hobbled down the grade, hearing the iron squeal of the wheels of a train coming from behind, I only worried that the train would follow me into the tunnel before the drone did.

Then I heard a woman's scream coming from the station behind me, a sure sign that the Drone Junior had revealed itself when it couldn't find me the easy way. I stepped into the first safety and glanced around the concrete corner to see that Junior had entered the tunnel with three banks of LEDs glaring right, left and center, and the glint of the train headlight just coming down from the higher tunnel behind it. There wouldn't be enough time for me to go the next two hundred feet, but another tactic occurred to me.

I jumped out into the middle of the track, being careful not to fall over onto that blasted third rail, waved both hands, and jumped back into the safety. The single slug that whistled past and down the lower middle of the tunnel told me that Junior—or its operator—had seen me. To be sure, I stuck out a hand and pulled it quickly back into the safety, no slower than a snake poking out its tongue. This time a slug bit into the concrete corner and sent crunchy bits scattering back onto the track.

The grind of the 'L' car's motor and the light from its headlight started to light the tunnel walls like the moon coming out from behind a summer cloud. Under that, I could barely hear the buzz of Junior approaching my alcove. No further provocations were necessary, just a little patience and a whole lot of luck. The floor of the tunnel started to shake with the approach of the train, and then I heard a slight hesitation in the buzzing of the drone's rotors. Was this the depth where it lost its signal?

I flattened myself against the back of the safety, as far away from the oncoming subway cars as I could get. If the drone lost its signal and crashed under the wheels of the train, success would be mine. If it didn't and flew up and over the train, I'd still have to endure the sudden rush of pressure and air as the train passed me before I could make a run for it. I should have closed my eyes to keep the dust out of them, but I couldn't force myself to do it. I didn't want to be shot by Junior with my eyes closed.

So, just at that moment, Junior pulled to a stop abreast of the safety alcove and turned to give me a good look. No sooner did it turn than I heard a click, then another. Somehow, its firing mechanism had jammed. Maybe it was loss of signal. Maybe it was just dumb luck. The roar of the train and the mini-earthquake of the shaking floor reached a crescendo as the first car crashed into Junior and sent it careening down the tunnel ahead of it. I could hear the train operator apply the brakes while another sound, something like that of a wire basket bouncing down a rocky hillside, came from down the tunnel ahead of the slowing train.

It wouldn't be the last time I spent the whole night in a subway station. Once the smell of oil and ozone stops assaulting your nostrils, it's replaced by a background of urine and a periodic intense olfactory raid by slowly drying vomit. When the 'L's are running, all is swept away by the air that rushes into the station with each train. If it's a humid, summer day, the rush is like steam billowing from a boiling pot of dirty socks. In the winter, it's as if someone opened a refrigerator in which all of the contents had spoiled. I know that indigents sleep in the subway, and, if they can do that, then I guess I'd have to pity the poor brain that has to turn it all off even if it's with the help of a cheap half-pint or a dose of some rotgut concoction cooked up in the back of an abandoned garage.

A second after the train had hit Junior and the operator had hit her brakes, she was on the phone to her dispatcher and then to her union rep. If it had been a six-car or an eight-car, rush-hour train, I might have been trapped in the alcove until she or her supervisor decided to move it. As it was, however, the train completely passed me before it came to a full stop, and I slunk away up the tube back to the station as a half a dozen confused and angry passengers peered out the back windows wondering who I was. So there I sat on a bench, taking in the aroma of a Chicago subway and wondering how long it would take some rookie uniform to come down the stairs to the platform and arrest me.

It must have been a bad night on the streets, because the FD came downstairs first. Taking little notice of me, and shoving the other scarce customers on the platform aside, the firefighters carried tanks of fire suppressant on their backs and communicated by radio with what I was able to gather was another FD brigade walking the tunnel from Harrison Street. Then came the transit super, a greying man with bags the size of baby dills under both eyes, and just as green. He wore the usual identification and carried an operator's satchel so he could run the train out of the tunnel and get traffic moving again. Close on the super's heels, the union rep appeared wearing the obligatory jacket with the local transit union logo and a pair of dress slacks from Carson's. "I need to speak to my sister first," the union rep, who was black, yelled at the super, who was white.

The super spun around with the ease of a figure skater to walk backwards and snapped back, "The hell you will!"

I thought I'd give the rep a break, and, besides, I knew that there'd be a cell phone or a radio or both with the super. "Supervisor Barnett!" I called, scanning the name tag quickly. "I need you to get a message to Superintendent Garrity."

He stopped in his tracks and let the union rep continue towards the tunnel. Garrity was the police superintendent I told you about at the beginning of this story, Chief Terwig, or more correctly Aloysius Terwilliger Garrity. "An' who might you be?" asked the supervisor, now interested.

I thought of showing him my credentials for a second, but guessed that he might need more motivation. "I've got info for him that will get your tracks open a lot faster."

He reached into the satchel and pulled out a multi-band radio as he asked, "What might that be?"

"Tell Garrity that Charlie Komensky says the attack on the Museum Park high rise and the crash in the subway are part of the same incident."

"Why don't you tell him yourself?" The voice came from the stairs as Chief Terwig and his entourage landed on the platform. "Somehow, I knew this had your prints all over it, Charlie." The overweight and out of shape police superintendent, wearing a brown overcoat that looked too warm for spring, strolled up to my bench and sat down heavily beside me, leaving two uniforms and his pipsqueak of a press secretary named Sveltheimer to stand and hover. "Sorry to hear about Linda," he added as sincerely as I'd ever heard from the likes of Terwig.

I truly didn't know who else I could trust right then, but I knew I could trust Terwig. I could trust that any action he took or ordered taken would be face-saving for the department first, and in his best political interests second. But I'd never known his political interests to cross the line into gross criminality, just over the margin into the kind of graft that was expected of Chicago politicians. And I knew he had justifiable distrust in the Department of Justice, as he did in most federal law enforcement. Through his many years with Chicago PD, he'd seen too many high-profile cases hijacked. Back when I was on the force, he had aspired to executive work with the FBI. For him, it must have been like the hammer of some Norse god coming down on him every time he was close to closing a case that would net him the rep he needed to move on up to the big time. His anvil had been beaten on so many times by the feds that, by that spring, Terwig wouldn't have taken a federal directorship if it came with a free ticket to heaven.

I guess what I'm saying is that I trusted him about as much as I trusted anyone, and all that a phone call to Doug had gotten me was attacked by drones. If I played my cards right, I could, at very least, predict what he would do.

"So tell me your side of this mess," he said as he put one hand on my shoulder and shooed the transit super and his radio away from us with his other.

"Everything you need to know is on this video." Why hold back? I would drop the thumb drive into his lap. "For his or her own protection, don't ask me to reveal the source just yet. Just know that it'll hold up in court if that's a concern." Sveltheimer stepped in front of us and held out his hand for the thumb drive. I suppose that's what any ass-kisser would be expected to do, hold onto the evidence for the chief and turn it over to the appropriate district commander. But Terwig looked me square in the eye and asked the silent question: How important is it that this stay between us? I barely shook my head no. Terwig glanced at his assistant, looked quickly back at me, and then, in plain sight of everyone, dropped the drive into his overcoat pocket. By that simple gesture, he told every one of his subordinates that this information was only for him to know, and that was that. I had trusted the right man.

As if by the power of telepathy, the feds showed up a scant minute after that. I suppose I should have expected it; I'd touted the evidence in my message to Doug so tantalizingly that he might have let his contacts at DHS know what was going on. Too much about what Doug did those days was out of the realm of what I considered good sense and logical detective work. However, as I later learned, a district commander who would be in line for Terwig's job, reasoning in his thick, bureaucrat's skull that the subway incident involved an "aircraft," called in the feds out of spite and a misplaced confidence that he wouldn't get blamed for screwing things up if the feds took a lead role.

Terwig did me the additional favor of telling the feds I had already given a statement—they could have a copy in the morning—that I had been innocently taking the subway home because I had a few too many, and all I saw was the drone whiz down the tunnel followed by the 'L' train. Then he called his detectives over at Beth's place and asked them to keep her statement under wraps for the time being. It would be only a matter of time before security cameras revealed the attack in the underground parking lot.

Whether or not they were Johnny-on-the-spot, it took the feds until 8 a. m. to analyze the debris from the drone. Terwig shared the results with me at 8:15, and I learned later that WGN News carried it by 8:30.

The drone—Terwig insisted on calling it by its accepted acronym UAV, for unmanned aerial vehicle—was a heavily armored model built in Ukraine and mostly sold to Eastern European, former Soviet-bloc countries that weren't part of NATO. The design seemed to follow known Russian influences. It masked its actual signal as digital frequencies that weren't supposed to be active, so at least that was a step forward in tracing the control signal. These small but deadly weapons came equipped with an unusual .20 caliber, high velocity round fired through an air-cooled barrel and a magazine capability of a hundred rounds. The federal techs said it wasn't a fully automatic weapon, but guessed the controller could get off something like two rounds a second. Since nobody in the U.S. was supposed to have one, including known police agencies, terrorist organizations, collectors and drone enthusiasts, the report presented no directions for further investigation. They'd have to go through diplomatic channels to get to the builder, with no guarantee that the builder would cooperate. To my dismay, the feds called in State and Central Intelligence, and I wondered why Doug Christie hadn't shown up to put the icing on the whole cluster.

After that, I made myself as invisible as possible as I skulked around the other end of the platform and stayed as far away from cops and agents as I could. The burn on my leg both smarted and throbbed, though my old wound pain had subsided. It couldn't have been good that the feeling in my foot hadn't come back, but I had to stick around to see if anything else hit the fan.

Then Georgio found me lurking in the shadows. "You look like shit!" was his honest greeting.

"Thanks," I said sarcastically. "Now I look like I feel."

On the other hand, as always, Georgio looked like he'd just been to the barber. "Here." He offered me a donut from a Dunkin box he'd brought down with him. I devoured it as we talked.

"How'd you get down here. I thought they had this cordoned off."

He shrugged. "I had two boxes of donuts when I got to the yellow tape. I thought you'd like to know that I tracked down the whereabouts of your Father Liebowitz."

"Good! Looks like that might be all I've got to go on for a while. Where is he?"

"Accordin' to my source, he's been allowed to take a "psychological sabbatical" at a rectory down in Kankakee. You ask me, he was ordered to do it."

"I didn't think priests were allowed to go crazy. Isn't that what they did with the pedophiles?" I sincerely hoped that my only lead wasn't in that group of nut jobs.

"If you'd start practicin' again, you'd know that it's also for members of the clergy who might need refuge from the authorities for other reasons." For some reason, Georgio felt the need to cross himself just then. "Look pious!" he hissed and nudged my arm. I realized at the last moment that a DHS agent had walked in my direction, but, because we were apparently praying together, he turned around and walked away. I'd seen it before. People praying in public frightened law enforcement like nothing else. That agent would have sooner walked into a brawl between two armed drug dealers than interrupt a prayer. "See?" observed Georgio. "It pays to pray."

"Georgio, my friend." I put one arm around his shoulders. "Get me the hell out of here."

CHAPTER TEN

G angland characters like Georgio Luchesse have to know a lot of things and a lot of people to survive on the harsh and deadly streets of Chicago. It's probably why the younger gang bangers and street gang member who are just playing at criminal enterprises die messy deaths in larger numbers than Mafia wiseguys.

I could go through the whole list of things a Mafioso needed to know, and bore the hell out of you, so I won't. What I will tell you is the top item of the list would be the names of all the contacts for the two hundred or so street gangs that seem to make up the "deadly" part. At the bottom would be what kids who were not in street gangs, kept their eyes open, and could be counted on to produce information on the flash of a twenty by any member of the Italian mob. An unwritten rule in Luchesse's circles, and with the Irish, the Russians and the Serbs, was you didn't pop a kid for what he did and didn't give up, and you never threatened them for information. Not so with the street gangs, who distinguished themselves by their lack of rules and of morals, and their eagerness to shoot a five-year-old without compunction.

But back to the list. Somewhere in the middle were the three things you always could count on Georgio to know: Where to get good Italian food, where to find a poker game, and where to get medical attention that wouldn't call the cops.

My medical attention that morning was Dr. Craig Sparks, DVM, a vet who had lost his real medical license through no fault of his own when a partner in a pain clinic scheme got busted supplying controlled substances to the aforementioned "no rules" crowd. I hadn't told Terwig that I was hit by the other drone, the one that was still out there, and I decided that going to a real doctor left me a sitting duck for the feds when they realized that I might know more than either of us was telling them. I'd take my chances that Beth Pea would have the good sense to keep her beautiful, sexy mouth from flapping until I got things ironed out.

In the doctor's living room, we waited for what seemed like hours for him to sterilize the dog cooties off some instruments. I had a chance to bounce a few things off Georgio's noggin, the one that contained that magnificent list, and see if I was missing anything. "Who do you know that would have a fleet of armed drones like that?" I asked as Georgio was burying his nose in one of Dr. Sparks' '90s vintage girlie mags.

Without looking up he answered, "Nobody I know of."

"Stop slobbering over that spread and elaborate."

He looked up. "That UAV stuff is a little too impersonal for our guys." Meaning the Italians. "If we wanna off some guy, he's gonna know who's doin' it."

"Who then?"

He tossed the magazine onto a well-stained coffee table. "Same with the rest of the organizations. The Russians probably wouldn't mind having 'em, but just to play with. Maybe blow up a few parked limos. That kind of thing. Everyone else on the street is either too stupid or not stupid enough. The Mexicans are a one-trick pony; mass graves south of the border. If there's a Venezuelan mob, it's lost in the noise. Puerto Rican? Negatory." After some thought, he observed, "Seems to me it would take a whole lot of money and a whole lot of time to set something like that up. With manpower literally oozing down the gutters around here, it's not like we gotta hire robots."

I reflected on Georgio's knowledge and experience, and the fact that he had been a mob informant, effectively a double agent, since the Italians recruited him at age eighteen. "You make a good point."

While the pooch doc was icing my leg and taking care of the infected burn from the laser blast, I thought more about it. Even with a couple hydrocodone in me, the known facts were clear as a bell. Doctor Marco Cajo had been killed in an explosion initiated by a rocket fired into his laboratory from a drone aircraft, a UAV if you will. As a direct result, another staff member was killed by gunfire. A prime suspect, my Linda, was arrested and charged under Patriot Act rules. Dr. Cajo had, in fact, kept something in his safe that he reported to be artifacts obtained in Venezuela, which was also his birthplace. That the artifacts existed was doubtful, as even his closest associate at the museum had never seen them, they had never been presented in any scientific way, and the people who accompanied him on his trip to Venezuela could not be found. Going down that path, I reasoned that the contents of the safe could be anything but artifacts: Drugs, tangible valuables, stolen information, evidence sufficient for blackmail.

Another thought of Linda intruded. She had almost lost her life on my last case, and it had been Georgio who helped me save her. Linda! My Linda! Maybe the drugs were having an effect. A feeling of woe and hopelessness, followed by a wave of fatigue, swept over me. I had to fight to recover my focus and stay on track. I could hear my heart pounding in my chest, and the pressure that welled up in my head started my ears ringing. Here I was flirting with death and a sex addict, and that didn't honor Linda's memory at all. Stay on track!

Shaking it off, but not really shaking it at all, I remembered that something else was clear—almost a fact. What I had told Doug in my message: Linda couldn't have been behind using a drone, an expensive and highly sophisticated weapon, to conduct a domestic terror assassination. I needed to know who controlled those drones, so I needed to know what Father Liebowitz, now of Kankakee, knew about it. Maybe Fr. Liebowitz also knew who Cajo was blackmailing.

I didn't like the looks of the police tape still strung across the entrance to the Museum Park parking garage and told Georgio to get the hell out before the feds realized I was in the area. It was probably for the better. My old wreck of a salvage car could have left me on the road somewhere in Manteno, and, being the natural-grown train nut that I am, I preferred to take the train. Besides, the 4:05 p.m. departure from Union Station would give me time to clean up.

Georgio hooked me up with a room in a dive on South State Street where the outfit held clandestine meetings and, a pay-by-the-hour hole sufficient for a hot shower and a shave. The place also served as a way station for Mafiosi needing a get-out-of-town-fast card. For two C-notes, the Rastafarian desk clerk provided a suitcase full of Salvation Army clothes in my size and another burner phone. After the shower, I chose a pair of nifty brown slacks, brown loafers, and a grey shirt with collar stays. My own jacket was still serviceable. For another fifty, the clerk brought me a box of .38 jacketed hollow points. He was used to doing it for the mob, so I figured why the hell not. If I went back home or to the office, I'd be a sitting duck. Either the feds would corner me and waste my time with needless interrogations, or whoever controlled the drones would try to finish the job they tried to start in Beth's apartment.

The train, still called the Illini as it had been when I was a kid, had, over time, become a sort of commuter train for all of the Illinois stops on the route of the more famous City of New Orleans. Carded for an hour and seven minutes to Kankakee, it made only one stop between. Packed with regular patrons as it was, it gave me little solitude to sit and watch the few cornfields that remained along the route go by. It's as if Steve Goodman somehow knew when he wrote the equally famous song about the City of New Orleans that the urban sprawl from the city of the big shoulders and fat ass would one day make Kankakee the last stop before the "houses, farms and fields" took over the landscape.

As I'd requested, Georgio had dug up "some people" with a car to take me to the Church of Saints Thyrsus and Projectus, and my objective. I think he was only half kidding when he said my driver's name would be Guido. They met the train, which was on time. Guido came with a black guy, and both looked like heavy muscle for whatever operations

Georgio's mob boss had down there. I sat in the back of their black Lincoln and watched the streets as they took me to a church in one of Kankakee's most rundown neighborhoods.

I tried offering cash for them to wait for me, but they refused to do anything more than drop me in front of the parish house and drive away. I figured okay, I'd cross that bridge if Fr. Liebowitz or one of his cohorts wasn't Samaritan enough to drive me back to the station. I could use the burner phone and call Georgio even if Guido and Tyrone didn't want to come back and get me.

The church complex occupied a city block, with the old, stone church facing east and the front door of the rectory facing west. The block across the street appeared to be fifty percent empty and twenty percent boarded up. A couple black kids slumped on one rickety front porch, not looking like they wanted to do anything but watch the white guy who just got deposited in their midst. If Kankakee had trash service, this neighborhood had forgotten to pay its bill. Paint and weed killer were both forgotten luxuries. I gave God a little thanks for Daylight Savings Time, and strode up the front door of the rectory. I knocked once, and a little shower of paint chips peppered my shoes.

Where the doorbell button had been on the outside casing, only a worn circle, a hole, and two dangling wires remained. Striking the two copper ends of the wire together got me the desired effect; a chime worthy of a church rectory boomed from inside. Still, no one answered the door. I gave it another shot and count of fifteen. Amazing! Nobody at home to accept a donation! The parish must have been flush. Then I decided I'd better go find out if Fr. Liebowitz or anyone was in the church.

An old concrete sidewalk ran around the south side of the rectory past a gravel and dirt driveway and a stone garage that looked like it had been built as a small stable. Behind the rectory, I found a Buick and a Chevy parked perpendicular to the drive and concluded that somebody should be home. The parking lot that I imagined to be full on Sundays sort of surrounded the back of the church in a U shape, but no cars graced it that evening. On the street beyond the church, I could see a van with tinted windows and a tinted license plate frame such that the plate couldn't be read in daylight. I knew that drug dealers and pimps on the streets of Chicago often utilized that deceit, but there was no telling in a town like Kankakee. I shivered as a gust of wind rustled the branches of the large, old trees. Rain would be moving in off the western prairies; the clouds had already dimmed the sun and accentuated the dinginess of the neighborhood.

I had gotten halfway to the back door to the sacristy when a gunshot issued from inside the church. It made me stop, duck, and draw my .38 even though I was in no immediate danger. The expected sound of running feet and the door of the van sliding open did not materialize. In fact, the neighborhood remained quiet; even the two delinquents didn't budge from their front porch. I took my time getting to the sacristy door, but nothing happened to reinforce the shoot-and-run I'd imagined.

On a gloomy scale of one to ten, I'd have to say that the sacristy of Saints Thyrsus and Projectus rated an eleven. As in many small Catholic churches in small towns all over America, the sacristy comprised the back part of the sanctuary. Built as a kind of lean-to, almost an afterthought buttressing the altar where a larger church would have chapels, the sacristy was just a rectangular room with no windows, a door on each end leading to the ambulatory and nave, and lined by a row of cabinets with counter tops on one long side and closets along the other. The only light came from a nightlight plugged into an outlet above a counter and from the red exit sign above the door I had just entered. Ghostly apparitions of vestments hung in one open closet, and a couple of empty sacramental wine bottles stood near the nightlight. One of the doors to the ambulatory stood ajar, and I listened carefully for any sign of movement in the church.

Hearing none, I carefully pulled the door wider and peeked into the church. The little light filtering through the old stained glass did nothing to fill the dark corners and spaces behind and between each row of mahogany pews. At the back of the church, I could see three or four candles lit at a shrine to one of the odd saints. Still hearing nothing, I called, "Father? Sister? Is anybody here?" But all I heard was a car starting, maybe the van I saw, out on the street.

I moved quickly down the side aisle and past the shrine, at which time I tripped on the man that lay in the back aisle, catching myself with my left hand on the back of a pew. As much as I wanted to run out the main portal and confront whoever was out on the street, I knew the man on the floor might need help.

The man was positioned on his side with his back against the foot of the shrine. I felt for a pulse, but found none beneath the man's white cleric's collar. Rather than hunt for a light switch, I lit a few more candles and held one in my hand to get a better look. A pool of blood had spread under his right arm, but not enough to indicate that his heart still pumped. The bullet wound looked like a .38 slug, right over the sternum, and the singed edges of his black shirt around it suggested the round had been delivered at close range, possibly by somebody who had come in the side door unexpectedly. I could see it in my mind: The door had suddenly opened and the priest stood up from his prayer, confronting the assailant and asking what he could do to help. The assailant produced a gun, fired a single round, surprising the priest, who in his last heartbeat staggered backwards and fell in the position of his death.

I shivered again, but not from the cold this time, and crossed myself, something I almost never do. What was happening here? I knew I should call the police, but I also knew that it would take hours for them to verify that my .38 wasn't the murder weapon. Reluctantly, I found the priest's wallet and checked for identification. The Illinois driver's license pictured a man about my age with dark, curly hair and an engaging smile, and identified the latest victim of this crazy investigation as Fr. Isaac Liebowitz, 45, of Chicago.

I checked his other pockets and found nothing except a piece of paper torn from a writing tablet with a seven digit phone number, judging from the prefix, probably a cell phone. But Fr. Liebowitz didn't have a cell phone on him.

Keeping a corpse company isn't one of my favorite things, and keeping one company in a dark church by candlelight went to the bottom of the list faster than a blood donor with HIV. So I sat on the hard pew and had a conversation with Fr. Liebowitz about how he could have tried to stay alive long enough to tell me what he knew. Then I thanked him for taking care of Linda's body, and for whatever else he had done during his priestly existence. I started to discuss the case with him, then realized that it wasn't impossible that somebody was listening or recording in there.

Over and over, for almost an hour, I carried the scenario of the shooting backwards in my mind to see if it took me to any answers. It had to be that I was not the only one looking for Fr. Liebowitz, and it was not impossible that whoever it was had access to the same resources that Georgio had tapped to bring me to Kankakee. Or . . . that person had somehow found out that I was on my way to Weird Saints parish and gotten here before me—just before me. Georgio knew where I was going, and he had a good head on his shoulders. He wouldn't intentionally reveal where I was going, unless it was to somebody he thought I trusted.

The only possible conclusion: Whoever killed Marco Cajo, whoever controlled the rogue drones, thought the priest had enough information that he needed to be prejudicially silenced. For some reason, they also thought the same about me. Whether by UAV or by minion, whoever it was had no compunction about killing a priest. Where the hell was everybody else in the parish?

The darkness, the quiet, the wind outside the church, my lack of rest the night before, and the repetition of the scenario all conspired to put me to sleep. I dreamed that I was running down a dark, Chicago alley with a laser-wielding drone close on my heels and Linda running at my side. In the dream, Linda suddenly screamed and was replaced by Beth Pea, running beside me, wearing nothing but a silver chain that held a large crucifix and her ID tag from the museum. Almost instantly, in the dream, I tripped over a pile of corpses, all dead priests, whose bodies suddenly stretched as far as the eye could see in all directions. Then laser drones closed in on me, firing on me with swift, orange fireworks.

Someone with rough hands holding me under the armpits and putting a black sack over my head interrupted the barrage just as a dream laser blast caught me in the side. I struggled to get away and to see if I was still dreaming—I wasn't—and soon found myself on my feet with my wrists in cuffs behind me. A low, not unpleasant male voice instructed my captors. "Take him," it said. "And be careful with the good brother's remains."

Once in my captors' car—I could tell by the way I had to be stuffed into the back that it was a sedan rather than a van or SUV—I tried to use the old trick of remembering stops, turns, acceleration, and so on, but to no avail. I tried to talk to my captors, but no response was forthcoming. They must have injected me with something while I was asleep, because after the second stoplight, I fell into a sleep that felt deeper than the coma I had come out of less than ten days before.

CHAPTER ELEVEN

"I'm hungry as hell in here!" Nobody seemed to be listening, so I yelled again. "A little food here!"

I found myself in a room I can only describe as monastic. I woke up from my long sleep on a comfortable enough bed, but one only wide enough for a child to roll over on without falling onto the concrete floor. The walls of the room were plastic-coated pressboard seamed together with some kind of polycarbonate spline, like the interior of modern mobile homes. Likewise the ceiling, except for a heat or ventilation duct and a clear plastic, rectangular panel, behind which a florescent light provided illumination. Where a cell in a monastery would have had a single window, a digital display, splined into the wall to make an unbroken surface, showed a picture of a meadow in which a shepherd dressed in modern clothes watched over a flock of sheep. I couldn't determine whether the picture was live or recorded, but it hadn't repeated since I woke up. Some kind of "sheepcam."

The only other furnishings were a fold-up wash basin with a toilet under it, a dresser, and a night stand with one drawer in which a Holy Bible reposed. I checked the little red ribbon, which was stuck at James 5:12, for any clue. I read, "But above all things, my brethren, swear not, neither by heaven, neither by the earth, neither by any other oath: but let your yea be yea; and your nay, nay; lest ye fall into condemnation." Good advice, but as for a clue?

I threw the Bible on the bed and tried the door. It was locked, but it was a plastic hollow core thing that I could have rammed down with one shoulder. The fact that my watch, wallet with twelve dollars in it, identification, holster and loaded gun, and all the ammo I had had in my pocket were on top of the dresser told me not to. Somebody wanted me to know they trusted me.

"Food! Please!" The only thing I had had since two donuts from Georgio was a moderately stale egg salad sandwich from the snack vendor on the train. My nine-dollar digital watch with the display that the Chinese made a billion of from stolen chips said 6 a.m. Central Time. I had been asleep for twelve hours unless my watch had been reset. If reset, I could be in a lot of places, depending on the mode of transport. Maybe London; the sheepcam seemed particularly English. Moving my jaw to pop my ears convinced me that I hadn't, in fact, been on an aircraft; otherwise, there would have been some residual pressure or pain from sleeping through the altitude changes.

The pastoral scene on the wall didn't change, and nobody responded to my request, so I washed up, splashed some cold water in my face, and took a dump. I had just put my watch and holster back on and pocketed my wallet and ammo when someone knocked at the door.

"It's your door!" I called. I guessed that drawing my gun wouldn't be much of a return on the trust thing.

"So it is." The voice, a little gravelly, sounded very British. Maybe I was wrong about the flying. A key ground in the cylinder, the door opened inward, and a man in his fifties with a long face, slightly angry eyes, brown hair done in an early Beatles, and a thin-lipped smile stepped in. The man wore a monk's hooded robe, open at the neck, and tied loosely with a white rope. "You're invited to breakfast with Master and Commander, Detective. If you are ready, I'm instructed to have you follow me." He turned without waiting for a reply, leaving the door open for me to follow behind him.

"If this is about what happened in the church," I said, since the idea that this was a monastery had been reinforced by the man's clothes. But the man or brother or whatever Christian mumbo jumbo he was just kept walking down a long hallway that could have been the inside of just about any office building in any city around. "It wasn't my fault." I still got no answer.

We reached an elevator door that stood open. Once inside, I noticed there were six buttons on the panel, all of which had a Christian cross on them, but no numbers. Brother "no talk" pressed the third from the left, and the doors closed. Though disoriented at the time, I still think to this day that the elevator moved sideways, or a combination of sideways and down. "Who's this commander?" I asked, but the monk, or whatever, remained silent. "Vow of silence, huh?"

The elevator doors opened onto a scene that, at first, struck me as being much like a prison dining hall. The much larger room before me had a two-story ceiling with a mezzanine surrounding it on all four sides. Wooden tables ran the length of the rectangular room with wooden bench seating provided. Along one wall, a cafeteria-style serving area doled out food to about twenty men, some in robes like "no talk," some wearing business suits, and other still in shirts and jeans. I noticed immediately that those in jeans had side holsters with Smith & Wesson M&P9c lightweight polymer chassis 9mm handguns. What the hell kind of monastery was this?

At the far end of the room, a long table ran crosswise; and, at the middle, sat a balding, jolly looking man in his sixties who was plowing his way through a four-egg, cheese omelet. He wore a tan, houndstooth sports jacket with a black bowtie, on which he'd managed to spatter a bit of melted cheddar. To my surprise, my guide walked right up to him as I followed. "Commander Morgan. This is Detective Komensky."

Commander Morgan stood up and offered a handshake. In a booming voice that didn't fit his appearance, he greeted me warmly. "Mr. Komensky. It is a distinct pleasure. Come! Come around here and sit down. I'll have Brother Fay get you a breakfast. I hear you're famished. Anything you want." I was speechless; didn't know what to ask for. "Brother, load him up a plate and be ready to come back for more!"

When I had made my way around the table and took a place on the bench at Morgan's side, I took a look around. Up on the balcony, what I thought was stained glass was another set of HD monitors piping in the pictures of stained glass windows. Morgan saw me looking and said, "We're eight stories underground here."

"In what building?" I expected we were in the sub-basement of one of Chicago's skyscrapers.

"No, no! This is the building. Eight stories underground." Morgan spread his hands as if blessing a congregation, and I noticed that a large, filigreed red cross adorned the pocket of his white shirt.

"And you're the commander of what, exactly?"

Just then, my huge tray of plates with omelets, bacon, toast, potatoes, meats and condiments arrived. There was also silverware bearing the same filigreed cross I'd seen on Morgan's pocket, and white linen napery. He said, "I'll give you a few minutes to refuel. Then we'll talk."

I have to admit, the breakfast smelled good, tasted even better than it smelled, and, for a cafeteria situation that obviously was in the habit of serving a large volume, excellently prepared. And you couldn't have found a better cup of coffee outside of Chicago's Greek Town. I've always been accused of lingering over my food, but, on that morning, I wolfed it down and started in on a second tray that appeared at my elbow. All during this time, Commander Morgan conducted his business with various subordinates in hushed tones. It gave me an opportunity to see that Morgan also carried a side arm, and that his armed members certainly looked and acted the part of well-trained members of some kind of military organization. Attempting any kind of escape by force would be tantamount to suicide. It boded well that they let me keep my gun and did not see me as a threat. But the mouse gets the cheese before the trap is sprung.

As I wiped the crumbs of well-buttered toast off my face, I turned to Morgan and asked, "So are you going to keep me here indefinitely?" During the meal, I had also spotted remote controlled security cameras at strategic points in the room.

Morgan turned away from the man who had been seated next to him, a burly young man with a wrestler's build, and addressed me. "No, Mr. Komensky. May I call you Charlie? Seneschal Hearst will take you back topside whenever you like. We just hoped you'd give us a listen first."

"You could have called me for that. Just Google me."

He sighed. "At that moment, unfortunately, you were in grave danger, and we had no contingency planned to move you anywhere but here." Then he added rather sorrowfully. "Which is what we'd intended to do with Brother Liebowitz."

"Brother? He wasn't a priest?"

"God forgive the deception." He crossed himself. "However it made it easier to get around little nuisances like the bond of the confessional." He paused as if reliving a painful memory, then asked, "Do you know who we are? What this place is?"

"I'm going to go out on a limb and say you're a Christian militia, a military order, or something like that. Or at least you think you are."

"And I'm going to ignore the obvious disdain you show for the Catholic Church." Morgan scowled.

Back then, few things riled me more than a so-called religious person spouting pieties about the church. I'd learned early in my police career that criminals stood behind church and God like both were some kind of magic shield to protect them from answering for their crimes. Despite my good mother's protests, I'd given up on going to mass after my father was killed, and the reader will remember that I was just as surprised as anyone that Linda Chelwood turned up Catholic. I stood up to make my point. "So you think that gives you the heads up to take out Dr. Cajo, frame my fiancée, and get her killed?" My raised voice called attention to the situation, and Seneschal Hearst and others looked like they were ready to draw their weapons.

"Hold!" Morgan made a dismissive gesture signaling that everyone should calm down, and then turned to me. "You've got us mixed up," Charles. "God bless you for calling to my attention how the situation looks to you, but you've got us wrong."

I sat back down. "That's what every criminal I've ever arrested had to say."

"Charles. Charlie? It always helps us to remember that even the best of intentions can be taken the wrong way. Will you let me clear it up?"

There was something about the guy that really was calming, charming. "Let's hear it."

"First let me tell you about Brother Liebowitz," he began. "Liebowitz was a recruit from Israel, an Israeli Christian who had been an active Mossad agent for some twelve years when he came to us through our network in the Middle East."

"A recruit in what, exactly?" I asked impatiently.

"I'm coming to that. The problem he was recruited to solve is one that has plagued the Catholic Church for some time now. Churches in the Middle East were not immune to this problem. In fact, Isaac Liebowitz had been a victim of this problem, and it is what compelled him to join us in our quest for a solution. It is unfortunate, but not entirely without precedent, that the quest cost him his life.

"Now to answer one of your questions. We are the Order of Montesa, or more to your liking, we think we are the Order of Montesa, as the Order, as well as its parent order, the Knights Templar, technically does not exist in the 21st century. However, just as in the Middle Ages, the 21st century Church needs a policeman . . . policemen. With the increasing secularity of governments, even in America, and the complacency of the Church hierarchy, we cannot rely on national, or even international police forces to solve the

Church's most tenacious problems. Governments want the Church to police itself, laissez-faire bishops agree with that, and do not want local police interfering with Church business. But the Vatican must not appear to use Gestapo-like tactics to get things done. After all, we are a Church of Peace.

"You may have already surmised that the 'problem' to which I refer is the tenacious persistence of abuse of children by Catholic priests and others of responsibility. Mind you, we've made great strides. But it had become ever more obvious to us, early in our quest for a solution, that there were outside forces beyond what we had imagined in the Person of the Great Destroyer, practical, worldly forces, and one in particular, that were turning our priesthood into a den of sadistic predators."

Commander Morgan paused in his story to let this sink in. I assumed he was referring to Cajo, and I still didn't see how that gave his order the right to play with Linda's life. So Brother or Father or whatever Liebowitz had felt guilty about them. So what?

"Ah, I see on your face that you've again jumped to the wrong conclusion," he continued. "Like Liebowitz, Dr. Marco Cajo was a friend of ours. But before I explain that, I'd like to introduce you to some of the other players." Morgan snapped the fingers of his left hand, and his seneschal produced a tablet phone and showed me the screen on which was displayed a picture of the inside of a large warehouse. Lined up in military order were rows of aircraft, drones, of a wide variety of sizes, degrees of armament, and weight of armor. "And, yes, the drones—we prefer the acronym UAVs, for Unmanned Aerial Vehicles—that attacked you and the rather licentious Miss Pea are from that arsenal. However, the armory was breached some six months ago with the loss—the theft—of some key UAVs and their control equipment."

He moved another picture onto the touchscreen. "This is Eduardo San Cristobal, a Venezuelan deacon who has become our arch nemesis and is responsible for the theft of those UAVs. Unfortunately, he is also misguidedly called Bishop San Cristobal, and is leading one of the largest congregations in Venezuela. Completely and utterly without portfolio, he has usurped both the Vatican and the faith of his followers and made a mockery of everything the Catholic Church stands for in Latin America."

I had heard of this man: An ordained deacon who had reportedly been inspired by a holy apparition to name himself a church leader. The sensationalized media were calling him the Unordained Archbishop of Venezuela—also UAV. Despite the efforts of the Vatican, both administrative and diplomatic, his close ties with the ruling party and with powerful financial interests allowed him to thumb his nose at the Papal emissaries. "If he's such a threat, why don't you take him out with your warehouse full of lethal toys?" I asked, but realized it was a foolish question. It would make San Cristobal a martyr and cement the power of people who shouldn't have it.

Morgan saw my concern and offered, "And martyr him? I don't know if that would be a good idea. But as long as he stays in Caracas, it is moot to speculate on a way to take him out."

"I'm surprised to hear the leader of a religious order speak so frankly about plotting murder." My experience had always been that the Church would shy away from any direct action against evil. Turn the other cheek, so to speak. That's why the Italian mob was so comfortable with the Church; they could confess anything and get a free pass to heaven's gates.

The Commander seemed contemplative as he ran his finger across the touchscreen, showing me picture after picture of the bogus bishop: San Cristobal celebrating mass, then greeting crowds of worshippers outside what appeared to be a cathedral-sized church. San Cristobal wearing vestments shaking hands with dignitaries, the Venezuelan president, party leaders. Again with businessmen, but this time seated casually around a table, smoking cigars, the only religious indication the suggestion of a clerical collar around San Cristobal's thick neck. Then San Cristobal once more, photographed with scantily-clad women on a beach, perhaps Rio, but still, himself, wearing his collar. "This evil man Cristobal is very vain," Morgan declared suddenly. "This last picture, with the skimpy swimwear, is as close as he will let himself come to scandal, but he photographs all of his abuses. He likes to watch his exploits, no matter how vulgar or horrific. We just have been unable to get any evidence. As I said, he is vain, but he is also very, very careful.

"Marco Cajo came to us a many years ago. Or rather he went to a parish priest, an honest man uncorrupted by this scandal that plagues us, and was then placed in the care of the Montesans. Marco had experienced San Cristobal's evil as a boy, firsthand, but didn't really let us know about the full extent of his knowledge until after he had conspired to make his archeological expedition to Venezuela. When he came to us, he was simply an orphan with an agonizing story of having been burned out of his home, such as it was, in the slums of Caracas. With the hope we always have of perpetuating the priesthood, the Order of Montesa educated him and brought him to America.

"While we were educating an archeologist who appeared to question God's plan, San Cristobal's brand of religion showed up more and more on our radar. The sudden uptick in the number of priests involved in child molestation and abuse caught the Vatican by surprise, but it was no surprise that the Montesans were tasked to find out what was behind it. Our investigations were thorough. The legendary leniency of the Church does not extend to this organization, Mr. Komensky, and does not suffer the lies of a fallen priest when the entire Body of Chirst is at stake.

"At every juncture, every turn of the page, every lash of the whip, every turn of the screw, every rape, every murder—and I'm not speaking metaphorically—San Cristobal came up as the one and only instigator of the literal network of evil, slimy, wretched beings who had somehow been convinced that the Church had robbed them of their 'sexual identity' and they had 'a right to express themselves' by having sex with children. And worse!" Morgan suddenly slammed his fist down on the table and made the breakfast plates and silverware bounce and ring like so many chimes. Every voice in the room went silent. The eyes of a hundred men looked at Morgan. Only when he shook his head, smiled and waved his right hand above his head did the assembly go back to their breakfast discussions.

"So the artifacts were really the evidence it would take to turn his flock against him and to put him away?" I asked the question, but I knew I was right. "And the evidence is now missing."

"That's what I wanted to ask you, Charlie." Morgan was less angry now, but more animated. "Are you sure what was in Marco's safe was gone before the explosion?"

"As sure as I can be. Not knowing that there weren't really artifacts in there, the crime labs may be testing for the wrong things."

Morgan reached out and took me firmly by the upper arms, his big hands gripping me earnestly. "You have to find out, Charlie! And you have to find out who has it. From what Marco told me briefly, those pictures show much more than you or I could imagine."

"I'm a PI, and I was a cop. You don't know where my brain his been."

Mass mutilations," he began. "Graves, sexual rituals, stabbings, blood, all involving children and adults."

"Okay, so my brain hasn't been there."

"And San Cristobal's latest adventure," added Morgan, slumping back into his chair. "Theft of the very weaponry we use when the shield of faith and the sword of the Spirit are not enough. I fear that, if San Cristobal can penetrate the Montesans and steal from us, we are done for."

I looked at him for a long time. Here was a man, maybe a priest—I couldn't tell at that point—who was in the business of telling others to put all their eggs in the basket of faith, and who was now telling me he had a gun taped under the basket. I couldn't tell what troubled him more, the breach of his cache of weapons, or a minion of Satan loose in his church. "I already have a client, you know. But I guess it's no conflict if I happen to recover the contents of Cajo's safe in the process."

"I wasn't offering to pay you." Morgan shook his head in disbelief. "I thought you would do it for the church."

"Uh, huh. Kind of a thousand-dollar bill in the collection plate, I guess?"

Looking sharply at me, he replied, "Would you rather that Evil triumph?"

I didn't really have an answer for that. My interest, first and foremost, was getting out of this poor excuse for a comic book hero's lair and start clearing Linda's name, and only second finding the bastard that started it. And if that meant nailing some faux priest for it, then so be it. "Okay, but you've got to level with me."

"I already have."

"Where are we? And what else was stolen from that arsenal?"

"You are in the Monastery of the Order of Montesa. And we—only we—will deal with what was stolen from our, as you say, arsenal."

"But. . ." I hadn't expected the Templar who came up behind me and swiftly slipped the injection into my shoulder.

Templars? Christian militias? The Order of Montesa? Did I believe these things or had this memory somehow been planted in my head? Like the revelations I had experienced when Georgio's serum had demolished the wall separating me from the repressed memories of my father, the mental images of the Montesans faded in and out, were clear and cloudy at the same time. If all my memories were a pile of lumber stacked horizontally on a floor, these memories would be boards that leaned vertically against the pile, moving from the front of the pile to the back with a will of their own. As I stood there in the middle of a fallow field, on a flat plain, with no landmarks to suggest my whereabouts, I didn't know how else to explain them.

The Montesans had left me with my gun, my ammo, my wallet, watch and fully-charged cellphone. If the watch hadn't been tampered with, another twelve hours had passed. The sun, about twenty degrees above the horizon and sinking, suggested that the time on my watch, 8:12 p.m., was correct, if I was still in the Central Time zone. My wallet contained an extra $2,500.00 in cash.

Because the phone had been a burner, its phonebook should have had only the few numbers that I'd entered during the train ride to Kankakee: Georgio and his Kankakee contacts, Doug Christie, Terwig's office, Beth Pea, my old police source Arnie Whittaker, and Linda. I'd entered Linda's first, out of a habit that probably wasn't going to stop anytime soon. When I thumbed the touchscreen to call for help, I found six other numbers I guessed had been entered by Morgan and his crew. They were labeled Morgan, Seneschal, HQ, Help, Strike-Ground, and Strike-Air; the HQ number being an international one I later learned to be an extension somewhere in the Vatican. Pretty impressive.

"Georgio." I practically yelled it when he picked up.

"Where the hell you been?"

"I was hoping you could tell me."

There was silence, and then, "The guys said they waited for your call and then gave up. We thought we'd find you dead in a cornfield."

"That's exactly where I am, but not dead."

"What cornfield?"

After a lot of swearing from Georgio, I finally found out, as sickly as my knowledge of the gadgetry available on a smartphone really was, that I could use the map service and GPS myself. With night coming, Georgio suggested I start walking to the nearest town. That cornfield, not in Central Illinois, but in Southern Minnesota, was going to get mighty cold in a few hours.

CHAPTER TWELVE

The adventure with Morgan and his militia at least had brought some clarity to the investigation. And I understood why it would have been a bad idea to take me back to Kankakee. This way, San Cristobal's people would have a hard time knowing where I was. I decided to stick with the burner phones, change every 48 hours, and never call anyone connected with the feds. That included Doug Christie. But I wasn't going to hide, either. Still couldn't rub salt in the wounds and go live at Linda's, but going back to my own little bungalow would have made me feel like Linda never happened. That'd be like rubbing salt in the wound and then rubbing the wound with sandpaper.

So, soon as I got back, I asked Georgio to check up on Doug, and I set up for as much research as I could do in my office in Oak Brook. I hung out a 'Closed for Remodeling' sign to throw off any of San Cristobal's men who might happen to show interest. Stole it from a store in the mall that wasn't going to re-open again anyway. A half dozen back issues of the *Trib* taped in the front window made it pretty convincing. The other three tenants in my condo office deal would just have to deal with my mess. As far as the temp secretary-slash-receptionist-slash-world-class-pro-text-messager, I came and went out the back, so she could honestly say she didn't know where I was. I'm not sure I really believed there were any other tenants in that dump.

I tapped into a little of the money I had left from the _Steam Locomotive_ case. I had a source I used in the hacker community by the name of Ops, whose legit handle was Unidigiac—for Universal Digital Access. This guy could hack the key code for the pearly gates if he had to, and without getting caught by St. Peter. I had him recommend two high-end Internet computers for me, and I had Georgio go out and pick them up along with my beater car and another handful of burner phones. The little bastard hacked into the computers almost before I plugged 'em in. In an hour, I had two laptops running on my desk with all the illegal software I'd need to find out everything I needed to know about San Cristobal, Templars, Montesans, sex crimes in Venezuela with Catholic connections, and Dr. Cajo.

It all boiled down to sex sometimes. We all have it, we all want it, and maybe Beth Pea's approach—just admit you want it more than what society thinks is normal and go for it—was healthier than even my limited inhibitions. But some of the stuff that came up on my monitor for the crimes part made me wonder if we would all be better off sterilized at birth. San Cristobal came up too clean on the surface, but with a strong undercurrent on the Darknet that he had something momentous to hide. It just jived with what Morgan had told me.

My motivation to solve the case felt stronger than ever before. I had no more nagging questions about Linda's innocence, even though why Cristobal targeted her remained conjecture. A convenient dupe? A chance meeting perhaps? Some connection with her mysterious ex?

As much as I had come around to Commander Morgan's way of thinking—according to my new research on Templars, "Master and Commander" was, indeed, his formal title—my priorities still put clearing Linda on a slightly higher plane than finding the evidence to "debishopize" the UAV, aka San Cristobal. If somebody other than San Cristobal or one of his minions had acquired the evidence, nothing out there showed it. San Cristobal couldn't have it, or he wouldn't have sent his stolen drones after me when I gave him the wrong impression by calling Doug about "evidence." Whoever had it, they were going to be patient and see how it played out between me and the bishop.

Okay, then. The dead janitor had been the next closest person to the missing evidence, and Eddie Figg, the security guard, had been the next closest. My new software made short work of getting a transcript of his statement, the secret grand jury, and the attempts being made by civil rights groups to turn the shooting of Laxalt Johnson into fodder for late-night and Sunday-morning TV and, hence, donations to their organizations. Figg wasn't going to talk before trial, and couldn't be approached. His attorney's confidential records had no mention that Figg held any evidence.

Don't let me fool you into thinking I mastered all the hacks, Darknet chat rooms, and sources for restricted information in a few minutes. Linda had spent months teaching me how to use the normal Internet, something I'd resisted with all my being. But learning this Darknet stuff was like a grizzly bear learning to use deodorant. Late afternoon on the third day, a message popped up from Commander

Morgan: "I see you've been digging into San Cristobal. Hope you're being careful. Any progress?"

PROBABLY CAREFUL AS A GAS EXPLOSION IN A COAL MINE, I answered.

"Don't worry. He can't see us here. We're on one of our servers."

THAT'S COMFORTING.

"Any more attempts on your life?"

I ATE AT DENNY'S THIS MORNING.

"Humorous."

IT GAVE ME GAS. MORE LIKE USING A CHEMICAL WEAPON.

"Yes. That's nice. I thought you should know that our intelligence has San Cristobal on the move. He left Caracas without fanfare. May be headed your way."

PEACHY. DO WE TELL THE ARCHBISHOP TO LOCK UP THE ALTAR BOYS?

"Not funny anymore. I'll do that. Just be careful."

YES, MY MASTER AND COMMANDER.

But nothing came back.

Charlie Komensky, Templar at Large. Had a nice ring to it.

Armed with another day's worth of lists of all known associates of Eddie Figg, and a little better idea of what to look for than when I was questioning Marvin Semolino, I had to get back out into the thick of it. It was time. Now I had a third mission: See if I can find Eduardo San Cristobal.

My gut told me that enough time had elapsed that he could no longer count on killing me in a dark alley and getting the evidence. I could have given it to a shyster by now, or put it in a safe deposit box; either way, it wouldn't guarantee him that the evidence wouldn't be out there to be used against him. Maybe I had a little bit of a life insurance policy there. On the other hand, that's all I needed was for whoever did have the evidence to step out of the shadows, and old Ed San Chris might just kill me for having the balls to confuse him. I guessed I had a window of a couple hours to a couple days, but I didn't really know.

Taking one of the laptops with me, I drove to a spot I knew on the access road where no security cameras could see me. Then I called Georgio to let him know what I was doing, dumped the burner phone in the ditch, and activated the next one, plugging in the xD card with my phone list. Finally, I pulled up my list of Figg associates. Most were either old school buddies, employees of the security contractor, or staff at the museum: Cooks, janitors, concession operators, etc. But one name stood out. I didn't know why I hadn't seen it when it came up. Danita Cambrero. I checked the source again. Damned social media. Eddie Figg had asked Cambrero out even though she was way out of his league, but he bragged on his Smackface page that she'd accepted.

I hadn't seen Cambrero since she'd left me dangling off the broken remains of the museum's third floor. Now I needed to find her. Kicking up gravel, I made a U-ie and headed back downtown to the condos across from the museum.

CHAPTER THIRTEEN

Although not my longest-running case, the museum murders—blast of murders or UAV murders?—was going on being a close second. Here it was mid-May already, and I'd cranked down the windows on the beater enough to get some 4-60 air into the stink of the seat upholstery. Whatever had been in that automotive piece of crud before it became insurance salvage, it smelled like a cross between full diaper pails and used motor oil. My usual ability to get to the crux of the matter early in the day held out in the usual way as I tagged late evening rush traffic all the way into 17th Avenue on the Ike.

The radio stuck on an AM talk station where some puke droned on about how Benghazi was going to be the downfall of civilization if some Democrats didn't start to tell the truth. I wanted to call in and tell him that civilization had already started its long slide into oblivion, and a politician telling the truth was going to be about as effective in stopping it as a speed bump in stopping an M1 Abrams.

Which got me thinking about whether me getting the goods on the Bogus Bishop was going to do anything about stopping the abuse problem in the church. The answer that popped into my head was a definite no, but it would go a long way to avenging Linda's death if this jerk was somehow responsible. I smiled at the thought of Linda and waved as a convertible full of college girls passed me on the left, laughing at the horrible mess I was driving. Another day, pretty college girls, another lifetime . . .

I should have known better than to drift off into fantasy land. The minor collision impact from a car pulling down the onramp to my right and behind me took me by complete surprise. I first thought, "Some schmuck!" But then the car, a late model Chevy, pulled behind me and I figured, "Let it go, Charlie. It's not like this piece of crap didn't have any damage on it." And I accelerated back up to 55. Checking my rearview, I saw that the Chevy had dropped back a little and was keeping pace.

Just past First Avenue the eastbound Ike makes a little jog to the left, which is when I noticed the Chevy coming up on me again and then falling back. "Drunk," I thought. We passed the Cook County building and I wished silently for a deputy to be on traffic duty ahead. The next exit was Des Plaines, and I thought about exiting just to get Chevy off my rear. As we crossed the river, there she was again, coming up fast. I floored it, but, like a tubercular racehorse, the clunker gave a snort and coughed up nothing in the way of downshift or extra speed. As a matter of fact, my speed started to drop and smoke clouded the rearview just as the Chevy came up matching my speed, connected with my rear, and then started pushing.

There's a cemetery on the south side of this part of the Ike, and the only thing that separated it from the traffic was a continuous Jersey bounce, except at the exits. Like the Chevy knew exactly where she wanted me to go, she suddenly gave a quick shot of the wheel to the left and my clunker started into a spin to the right, just grazing the east end of the bounce before it opened up and allowed me to go through about fifty feet of chain link and crash to a stop, nose against a seven-foot headstone that said, "Here lies Nicholas Binkersop, 1920 – 1999, A Very Good Man." If that clunker had ever had any air bags, the only thing left was the air part, allowing for a pretty good gash on my forehead and a bloody nose, and enough panic in my head to want to get out before an engine fire took me with civilization on the rest of the ride to hell. A real doozy of a headache started to nudge its way above and behind my eyes, and I had trouble focusing.

Luckily, my door still opened, and I was able to get out, dust off, and take inventory. I had landed far enough off the expressway that, unless somebody saw the accident, nobody was going to stop. I didn't know whether the Chevy had taken the exit to Des Plaines Avenue or went on east. Feeling around my shirt and jacket, I realized that the burner had been tossed onto the floor by the impact. Peachy, again. The smoke coming from somewhere under the firewall got more intense every second. Poking my head back in there didn't seem like such a good idea.

That's when she stepped from behind the headstone. I instinctively reached for my .38, but it wasn't there either, another victim of momentum. She raised hers, an almost identical .38 to the one I carried, and took a good bead on my forehead. The dust and smoke still made me blink, eyes watering, still hard to focus, and the pain in my getting worse. But I could tell she was a looker, this one. Tall and well proportioned, all encased in one of those leather suits that only female spies and Angelina Jolie wear in the movies, her hair hung long and jet black over her shoulders. The high-heeled boots matched the outfit, and leather driving gloves completed the cover. As a matter of fact, I could see only her face with two dark eyes looking at me over the gun. I blinked and tried to focus again. Pain pounded my head. She smiled. I started to go black.

Linda!

Some people break open an ampoule of salts to bring you out of a faint. A few of the cops I know slap the suspect in the face if they go limp during a hard interrogation. It happens all the time. Personally, I like a few licks with a wet rag to get them out of it.

My captor used a whole damn bucket of rancid mop water on me. I came to, soaked and startled, like a rabbit facing an unexpected pit bull. As soon as I blinked the sting out of my eyes, I saw that she had me tied to an old wooden teacher's chair—there seemed to be an endless supply of those in use by the criminal element—in some kind of warehouse; concrete block walls, high windows, empty racks where some product had been, and a smell like something died in a wall somewhere. My wrists were secured behind me with probably the same kind of nylon cord that held my legs to the chair. An additional twist was that she'd chained the back of the chair tightly to a steel post.

Once she put the bucket down and stopped laughing, a cruel, guttural laugh unbecoming of a woman so beautiful, she walked over to me. I realized that, despite my reaction back at the cemetery, this was not Linda. She looked like Linda, but the eyes were different, her nostrils flared in a way Linda's never did, and a small scar high over her left cheekbone marred her otherwise identical features. She had taken the gloves off, revealing a laborer's hands.

"I can see by the expression in your eyes that you have decided I am not your darling Linda," she said in English that had a pronounced Hispanic accent. At the time, I thought it might have been Puerto Rican. "What have you done with the evidence against the Black Bishop? And don't look at me like that! Just because I am not Linda, I do not need your pity!"

I looked her in the eyes and answered, "You've got it wrong, honey. I never had the evidence."

"*Mentiroso!*" She spat the word at me; I thought it might be a breed of dog. At the same time, she put her right boot against my chest with the spike heel dug into my sternum and the pointed toe under my chin, pressing just firmly enough that pain coursed through my whole torso. I became aware that the headache I had experienced before my blackout had not subsided, either.

"Sorry, sweetheart. As much as you remind me of Linda, and I'd like to help, same answer." She dug in a little harder, making me wonder if I could take another breath. "And, if it's all the same, I left my Spanish dictionary in my other pants."

She suddenly moved her boot down into my crotch and shoved. The pain was excruciating. "Perhaps I should make sure you never have anything in your pants." Just before I thought I'd black out again, she pulled her foot away and turned her back to me. "You *norteamericanos* will never understand what it is like in South America," she hissed.

I took a few seconds to catch my breath and let the pain subside. A heavy stream of drool ran down my chin, and I sucked it in, picked up my head and said, "This *norteamericano* didn't have anything to do with what it's like in South America. Unless I'm way off the track here, I'm guessing you're talking about Venezuela. Why don't you ask your boss? I hear he's trying to turn the country into one big fuck party."

"He's not my boss!" she snapped.

"Well, he sure ain't mine."

When she turned back towards me, her features had softened. I saw more of Linda in her eyes, but still couldn't get past the voice. She said, "You thought I worked for San Cristobal? I think I might have made a mistake."

"You bet you did, sweetie. Why don't you just take a look at that laptop you took from my car? You'll see that I've been trying to figure out who has the evidence, and I've got a couple pretty good ideas that you sorta upset in midstream. Then I'd appreciate it if you untied me and let me take a literally bloody piss!"

I watched her as she went over to an old, wooden desk next to the wall and started my laptop. "The password is OLIGARCHY," I yelled.

When she had finished, she walked back over. "I'm going to untie you now, please," she offered. "But please do not attempt anything rash."

I waited as I felt the cords release my legs. Then she bent over me, her breath hot against my neck, as she untied my hands. As soon as they were free, I stood up, clutched her neck with my left hand, and put my right arm behind her, pulling her to me until our noses almost touched. I whispered, "Don't ever do that to me again, sister." Then I couldn't help myself. I pressed my lips to hers and kissed her full, with all the pent up passion of the last few weeks, and with all the sensuality I had in me. She returned it for a moment, and then stopped and pulled away, not abruptly, as I would have expected, but gently, as though she really didn't want to. I let her go, watching the confusion in her dark eyes and trying to keep mine from showing the same.

She seemed to have become aimless, not knowing whether to address me or just leave me there, looking at this or the other, making a false start at going back to my laptop and learning as much as she could of what I had been researching for the past few days. "Would you mind?" she finally asked.

"Lady, as far as I'm concerned, any woman whose had a heel up my groin and lived to tell about it is on good enough terms to go through my computer. But just so you know, I only gave you the read-only password."

She pulled a folding chair up to the table and started hunting, so it looked like a good opportunity to see what information I could pull from her; the elephant in the room being her acute resemblance to my dead fiancée. "That you know what is missing from Cajo's safe," I started, not wanting to jump on the pachyderm right off the start line, "tells me you either knew Cajo or worked with him to get the information on San Cristobal."

She kept using the touch pad on the computer to scroll through my lists of lists of suspects and ignore my deduction.

"Am I warm?" I finally asked. "Or did you get that theory from Morgan?"

She turned suddenly. "Who is Morgan?" she asked, answering my first question.

"Morgan is irrelevant right now. But which was it? Did you help Cajo get the goods on your Black Bishop?"

Without answering, she cocked her head sideways, a little like stretching her neck, but it told me the subject was a painful one for her. Time to jump on the elephant. "I can't see you denying a relationship to my Linda. You've got to at least answer for that." Again no answer, so I kept talking. "Judging from your physical appearance, your apparent age, and near look-alike face, I'd make you out to be an older sister by just about a year, and maybe closer to the Catholic standard of one every nine months.

"Separated at birth might be too extreme to explain why you're showing up now, just when Linda has been accused of a terrorist act and then killed while in custody. I'd say more like your family managed to stay together until you were young girls, and then something, a tragedy, maybe, landed you both in an orphanage or foster care."

I'd learned long before then to check my surroundings while buying time with talk just interesting enough to keep someone a hair off guard. In this case, I scoped out the warehouse we were in well enough to realize that I had been there before. It was an old appliance parts warehouse that I had almost rented when looking for office space. Too expensive! The important thing was it was right down the road from Oak Brook Center, and my offices. "Then you were raised by the next worst thing to wolves, and Linda went to a nice family."

"Just shut up!" Her abrupt response startled me, and she stood up. I was just getting around to thinking that she had been the sweet thing in the sweats that dropped off the warning about Linda. She said, "Just shut up and let me tell you before you get everything wrong. Okay?"

When we were finished with that talk—she talked and I mostly listened—I regretted that her sister and I had never shared some of the things she revealed. And I regretted even more some of the things I'd thought about Linda over the years; things like growing up with privilege, being a little too conservative, sometimes being a frustrating bitch. I regretted the way I'd treated her, and, selfishly, I regretted that she'd never trusted me enough to share any of it.

After the talk, I knew exactly how Linda fit into the case, and why she'd been framed for the explosion that killed Dr. Cajo.

The sisters—they were, in fact, twins—had been born in America as Linda and Paula Langhoeffer, the only two daughters of a banker father of German descent, Henry, and a Venezuelan mother, Gloria, maiden name Asturias. When the daughters were twelve, the family traveled to Caracas. Gloria had some cousins there, and both she and Henry were genuinely interested in doing some charity work in the slums of Caracas. They were there two months when the parents were killed in an auto accident.

"That's the way he does it," Paula explained with an anguished look. "Sometimes he targets what he wants, and his men go out and cause an 'accident.' That's how he killed Linda."

I agreed that Linda's death didn't seem to be an accident, and that the authorities also didn't seem too interested in following up. But Paula insisted that it could be part of it, that the Black Bishop hired mercenaries to infiltrate law enforcement. It didn't have to be him operating the drones.

She continued by telling me the horrible way that they were yanked from their burning car while their parents begged to be rescued, and secreted off to a house where they were fed and clothed and allowed to recuperate from their relatively minor injuries, but always locked up or under guard. Then, she said, after a week of this, during which both girls felt that the people caring for them were both heartless and soulless, they were dressed up in white frocks and taken to a small chapel.

This is where San Cristobal "married" them in some kind of black mass. They were both drugged and laid out with their wrists and ankles secured on a raised platform. Paula had difficulty in describing the terrifying scene, and, thinking back, I'm surprised she hadn't blocked it out altogether. I'd had a little too much personal experience with blocking things out. Anyway, after they were stripped naked and touched and fondled by about fifty men, women, and children as young as they were, San Cristobal raped them in front of the gathered throng and then cut his mark into them. Then they were set free.

I told her that I remembered seeing a scar, but Linda had told me she'd had plastic surgery to correct something that happened to her as a child. I had never imagined.

The horrors of that day paled in comparison to what happened next. Alone, naked and lost in Caracas, marked in a superstitious society, completely unfamiliar with the language, they had no success in getting help. Twice more they were molested by people they asked for help. When they feared getting so weak they would die, they resorted to taking what they needed, leaving more than one poor soul bleeding in a gutter. Once clothed and able to get to a police station, they weren't believed. The American's had died, poor family, with their daughters in the car. San Cristobal had substituted children for whom he had no further use! One of the officers offered to "take them home." They ran.

The sisters resolved to become the ghosts that they then truly were. They started to learn the language, and, every day, they used theft and clever fraud to steal the barest essentials and to move ever further out of the city and into the Venezuelan countryside. Once out of the city, life became easier, people less cynical, more willing to give the benefit of the doubt. They went from town to town and farm to farm, offered themselves to women as household help and to men as companions and whores. When they found positions as nannies or maids in the homes of more affluent country landowners, they stayed, developed skills, and saved as much cash as they could lay away for that inevitable day.

As Paula told it, the savings never measured up to what they needed. To get back to America, they still had to rely on the South American underworld, which was male-dominated and unforgiving in its relentless sexual perversion, to get papers, documents, identification. Despite the disgusting side of their lives, the girls not only survived, but managed to build up quite a network of sources in South America. But in the end, by their twentieth birthday, only Linda could make the trip back to America.

Paula stayed in Venezuela for two more years, it was then 1989, and she kept in touch with Linda, who had begun the process of becoming a respected businesswoman in Chicago. Moving to Buenos Aires, Paula soon fell in love with, and married, the man who would become the father of the elusive graduate student of Dr. Marco Cajo.

Paula's son knew the whole story, unlike a certain private detective who had been left to fly blind all those years, and had been more than willing to help Cajo expose the Black Bishop for what he really was. Unfortunately, Paula's son didn't make it out of Caracas with Dr. Cajo, and hadn't been heard from since the expedition. She assumed he had been tortured for information, which was confirmed when she learned that Linda had been targeted and the contents of

Cajo's safe missing. After that, Paula could stay out of it no longer.

CHAPTER FOURTEEN

"Did you ever see the evidence?" came the first question out of my mouth. I'd been listening to her story and trying to will my headache to go away, not at all convinced that the crash hadn't aggravated the head injury from the museum a few weeks ago.

She looked stunned and drained as she answered, "No. I wasn't even there. I was in Argentina."

"If San Cristobal is as powerful and all-reaching as you say, how could anyone approach the authorities with it? How could even Morgan?"

"Morgan, again?"

I didn't think it was time to reveal the Montesans. "Nobody important. It's just that I'm not getting it. Unless that's why Cajo was taking so long getting the evidence out. Like Diogenes, he needed to find an honest man."

"Now Diogenes?" she questioned. "I don't know what you're talking about."

I suddenly realized that Paula hadn't had education beyond eighth grade. I had to stop thinking out loud. "It's a reference to Greek Mythology, Paula. But that's not important right now. If San Cristobal could find Linda, then he knows you're here, and you probably put him on to me, too. Did anyone follow us here?"

"I was cautious. The Chevy is stolen."

I grimaced at that, and then asked, "What about a cell phone? Did you leave your GPS on?"

She reached into a tight, leather pocket and pulled out a small Android. When she started to finger the screen, I took it from her and smashed it to the floor, sending fragments everywhere. "If you don't know if you had it on, you probably did. We've got to get out of here."

Paula hustled over to one of the desks, opened a small drawer, and withdrew two .38s, one of them mine. I could tell because hers didn't have the safety modification that had been added for me by a gunsmith down in Chicago Heights. (For those readers who have read the other books about me, I don't think the author bothered to mention that I used a modified .38.) She also had the burner phone that had been thrown to the floor of my beater in the crash. I readily accepted both, checked the .38, and clicked on the safety. The phone had been turned on all this time, so the battery was down to two bars; it would have to do.

"Look," I said. "I think I may know who has the evidence. But we're not going to be able to find out by remote control. We've got to get downtown."

The trench-coated figure that stepped sideways into the door and turned to aim a Sig P226 .40 at us wasn't strange to me, though she did surprise me. I saw Paula trying to make a slow move and stopped her by addressing the figure. "Agent Barry," I exclaimed with as much irony as I could muster. "You're out without a collar and tags again."

"Funny, asshole," she spat. "Both of you keep your hands where I can see them."

I knew now that Barry had been the agent who took a few shots at my office window. She'd been tailing Linda's sister. I nodded towards Paula and shot another barb at Agent Barry. "I bet you'd like to put your hands where she can see them, and maybe where she can't."

"Shut up! There's nothing stopping me from putting a slug in that smug face of yours, Komensky." I could see her face growing redder by the second. "You like to do things outside the box, smartass? Maybe I'll just put you in a shallow grave without benefit of a box."

"You're too good an agent for that, Barry." I tried to sound sincere, knowing that she was really just one of those cogs in the machinery that only did what her supervising agent told her to do. Even though I couldn't believe that she was in league with San Cristobal, anything was possible. "So what brings you here?" The entire time Paula had been inching closer to one of the metal racks where a small wooden crate sat. There was something metallic in it, but I couldn't see what, so I kept on with the patter. "I'm up for a threesome if you are."

Barry laughed, and snorted as she did so. "We just think it's kind of funny that you're consorting with this woman who looks so much like the museum bomber." She glanced at Paula, who stopped in her tracks with her hands up, then turned back to me. "I knew you were part of this conspiracy."

"Yeah, Barry. I had Linda cloned so we could bomb another museum. I woulda cloned you, too, but the cloning machine took one look at your picture and asked for a psychiatrist."

Paula's quick movement startled both of us, but mostly Barry. She'd thrown the crate full of black, half-inch ball bearings onto the floor, making a sound like a rattlesnake.

Most importantly, as they rolled in Barry's direction, they looked like so many roaches skittering in her direction. As she stepped back, I lunged in her direction, just getting enough grip on her forearm to force her arm up and deflect her aim towards the ceiling. I didn't have to do any more. The recoil from her discharge made her step sideways onto the rolling balls. Losing her balance, she fell head backwards against a table and landed in a twisted heap on the floor. I felt her neck for a pulse; there was a strong one, though a trickle of blood issued from her head wound.

"Quick," I said to Paula. "There's not much time before somebody else from the agency comes looking for her. This could mean that San Cristobal has people with the feds. They can't be trusted, so Cajo was right to hold his water. You okay?" I could see she was shaken.

"Good as ever."

The Chevy, even with the body damage, was the best car I'd been in since the feds had impounded Linda's and mine. Maybe it wasn't such a good idea to be driving a stolen car, but there were bigger worries. I told Paula to keep it with traffic and don't make any actionable maneuvers as we hit the Eisenhower again and headed downtown. She'd demonstrated her driving prowess in that little demolition derby twist by the cemetery, so I knew she could get us there while I placed a call to Georgio.

"Man! I was just about to send out the Praetorian Guard," he said in answering. "When I saw your GPS go back to Oak Brook from Broadview, I thought you might be in some kind of trouble."

When I explained I needed a "cleaner" to pick up Barry and put her on ice until this was all over, he got the general idea of just how much trouble.

"You know I don't want anything to do with making people go away," he explained. "Even for you."

"Nothing like that, pal. Just give Judge Burmeister a call. Once your guys have her in neutral territory, maybe he can talk to her and find out who in the agency is pulling the strings. You know most of the story, so give the old judicial fart whatever he needs to know to keep us from falling too hard when the shit hits the fan."

"Can do, Charlie. Where you headed?"

"Going to a sex party." I hung up the phone.

I did know that I still needed one more piece of the cheese to finish the whole wheel. As far as I was concerned, just finding and exposing the evidence against San Cristobal wasn't going to be enough . . . for me or for Paula. If the Black Bishop was in town, we needed to get him out in the open. The whole thing so far made sense. I'd have go all in and bet that, whoever had the evidence would try to do some Black Bishop blackmail.

For my taste, if I had been going to blackmail someone, it wouldn't be a rogue pervert priest with an army of followers and the covert ability to pick the pocket of an international militia. Any number of times, during the course of my career, I could have targeted somebody like a pipsqueak prosecutor or a two-bit mobster. With information gathering abilities, it wouldn't have been hard, and it would have been much safer. But blackmailers who aren't professionals are desperate people. If I did it, I'd do it for the extra spending money, not because I owed some drug dealer. This amateur was up against a professional who surrounded himself with professionals.

We rode along the Eisenhower Expressway in silence for a while, me lost in thought about who could have Cajo's evidence, Paula concentrating on traffic and occasionally biting her lower lip in frustration just like Linda used to. I got the impression that she wasn't used to abiding by speed limits. Finally she said, "I want you to know that I heard everything you told your friend on the phone. I was just, how you say, processing it."

"So how does it process, Linda. I'm sorry, Paula!" The slip had been unintentional and painful, and I winced. "How does it process?"

"The Black Bishop is a sexual deviant," she reasoned. "So we must become deviant to catch the deviant."

"Something like that. But we don't have to participate. We just have to develop a few contacts. Exit at Austin." I knew a party store there where we could buy a couple of harlequin masks and look just enough like participants who "like to watch" that we would fit in. I also knew Beth Pea would be having one of her fundraising events that evening. No matter how civilized and adult her parties, and I had no experience on that front, that didn't mean some of her guests weren't into other gatherings that would land them in jail. If sex addicts were like any other addicts, some would cross lines willingly to feed the addictions.

As we sat waiting for the green to make a right onto Austin, a police cruiser pulled up in the middle lane. The cop in the shotgun seat gave us a good looking over, but I figured it was Paula he was gassing. When the light turned green, we made our turn without being followed. "So why is you know where to find a sex party on short notice?" asked Paula as we drove south on Austin. The question sounded more like curiosity than criticism.

"I charge people a lot of money to know things, Paula."

"So we are going to buy party favors?"

"Just reel it in a little, doll. We're going to buy masks so we can remain anonymous. Lots of people go to these things and remain anonymous." Then I added, "Or so I hear." She nodded yes and kept driving. "I'll look a little grubby for it," I added. But you'll fit right in wearing that leather thing. Maybe just unzip the top a bit an' show what you've got on under."

"Who says I've got anything under?" Her grin said she was messing with me, but I wondered.

Chapter Fifteen

If Linda getting arrested, thrown in a DHS holding tank and probably tortured, and then killed while being transferred in custody would be considered a setback, then no. What happened the rest of that evening, after Beth's "gathering," might only be considered a minor annoyance.

The annoyance began as we left Beth's, and two CPD uniforms I'd never seen before dragged us out of the elevator, through the main lobby and, eventually, to police headquarters. They said we were wanted for questioning and didn't say by whom. I had a few guesses, but didn't share them with the officers, whose name placards must have been "dislodged" when they accosted us.

Chicago's police headquarters has more floor space devoted to management than does an average, Fortune 500 corporation. In spite of this, there are some fifty different interrogation rooms in the building, ranging from minimum security, where a battered spouse and children can be questioned without scaring the jeepers out of the kids, to a supermax kind of room where you could probably put Frank Abagnale, give him a full box of tools and a flame thrower, and he couldn't get out. It got a little too déjà vu for me when they threw Paula into one of the supermaxes, and then dragged me to a seat in an office with a window I could have jimmied and climbed out of at any time, one that belonged to some mid-level functionary I'd never heard of. Anyone who has read some of the stories about me knows that, when I get into trouble, the supermax is usually my norm. After questioning is over, so is getting released on my own merits.

But I'm getting ahead of myself here. The whole evening hadn't been a waste.

We had got to the party about 8 p.m. Surprised the hell out of Beth, who hadn't heard from me in a week or so. She looked disappointed, but I couldn't tell if it was because I'd showed up at something she wanted to keep me out of, or because I'd showed up with a sexy, leather-clad, unzipped-to-here stranger. All curiosity about these kind of events aside, Beth's appearance surprised me. Sure she wore a low cut magenta gown with slits down the side that showed a lot of skin in all the places you'd expect. She felt the need to explain that the hostess rarely participated in any of the "special games" that her guests expected, but she was, nonetheless, only human.

I explained that we just had to mingle with the guests, and that the purpose of our visit was not to compromise her fundraising efforts for the museum but to seek out anyone with information about the sex crowd looking for "harder" experiences. I think she knew what I meant. "Are you sure you're ready for this?" she asked me. Three times. I said I was.

I asked Beth if anyone I knew would be present, and, interestingly, she listed Danita Cambrero and Eddie Figg. Danita would be present out of duty to the museum, and Eddie supposedly because the lawyer the museum's insurance had hooked him up with had money and a leaning toward Beth's kind of party.

Even though I said I was ready for "Beth's kind of party," I wasn't. I have to admit that my old Catholic upbringing sprang up and hit me in the face as soon as I encountered a group, surrounded by onlookers, consisting of two semi-clad young ladies paying more than rapt tactile attention to an older gentleman's male organ. I supposed some guys get turned on by it, but I have to admit that I wanted to throw a blanket over the group so they could do it in private and lead all the watchers over the edge of the balcony.

I caught sight of Danita Cambrero on my second circle through the apartment. Buck naked, she stood holding a drink and talking to an equally bare young man with obvious attributes. She had the body I would have expected from our brief meeting at the museum, except for the strange blue tattoos, six of them, all consisting of numbers, letters and symbols. I didn't know what to make of it at the time, and avoided letting her know I was watching. Cell phone cameras were in use in every room. It appeared that the guests wanted to keep some very personal mementoes of the event, so I quickly snapped a few of Danita and walked the other way.

As I moved into one of the bedrooms I saw Beth talking to a short black man, maybe thirty, who was wearing a pair of tidy whiteys and a dog collar and nothing else. "Henry," she admonished the man, "tell the Jester here what you told me, or I won't beat you with the rolled up paper." I realized by Jester, Beth meant the mask I had on. It looked like the top half of something you'd find on a Vegas poker deck.

"Mistress Beth," said the man, acting the role of a confused puppy who maybe just had his nose rubbed in it, "I don't know that I should."

At that moment, Paula walked up on our little group and got right into the spirit. Towering over him in her black leather, the front unzipped to her navel, she ordered, "Tell us, little doggy, or I might not use the leather belt!"

"Oh, I don't know. I don't know," he whined pathetically.

"Tell us!" Paula's gloved left hand shot out and grabbed the guy's package like a python taking down a piglet. He groaned as his face turned ecstatic and she removed her hand. "No more until you tell us!" I noticed his whiteys were wet.

"Okay, look. I go to this other group, you know? And, like, the mistress there isn't as picky as Mistress Bethany here." He looked demandingly at Beth. "And, see, there's been this new guy. Dresses like a holy man, but he sounds, you know, foreign? And he keeps asking if there's ever going to be any boys and girls there, you know? Goodness knows I'd like to be, like, dominated by a child? As much as anyone, you know? But that would be wrong, wouldn't it?"

I towered over him now, and as I did so, he hunched over to make it seem like he was smaller, even, than he was. "When does the other 'group' meet?" I demanded.

"Thursdays."

"Where."

"If I give you the address, I'll be a bad, bad boy. Promise you'll reprimand me."

Beth spoke up. "I promise, Henry. Now be a good dog."

Once we had the address, a townhouse in Humboldt Park, and the name of the so-called mistress of the party, I took Paula aside. It had been all I could do to keep from slapping Henry into next week. But I guess that's what he wanted. "This stranger has to be San Cristobal," I told Paula. She nodded in agreement, but I noticed her gaze was focused on a couple copulating on a sofa. "Paula? This has to be him! The timing is right. I was sure a monster with tastes like his couldn't stay away from it. Even on a business trip to Chicago."

"So what are we going to do next?" she asked.

"We've got two days to see if we can find who has the evidence. So let's get out of here and start making plans." I took her by the arm to go, leaving what little respect I had left for Beth Pea behind. "And throw that glove in the trash on your way out."

The way out, as I pointed out at the beginning of this chapter, was in a cruiser on a direct route to police headquarters. As I sat in that bureaucrat's office, I couldn't shake the feeling that, unless I did something about it, Paula was going to meet the same fate as her sister. I tried to focus on some kind of plan. How much could I rely on Georgio and Judge Burmeister to provide manpower for an operation? Taking down San Cristobal and letting the rest of the world know why, particularly the good Catholics of Venezuela, seemed like it would be too labor intensive to work. I needed a tactical team, and I needed to find the evidence.

Presently, three men filed into the office. Did I just say presently? Holy crap! I've been writing this story so long I'm talking like a writer. When I'm through, I'm going to have to go out on a three-day bender just to make sure my brain is clean.

I should have said that I watched three mooks come in, and I knew all three. The first one didn't surprise me. The Superintendent of Police strolled in, trying to look confident while wearing one of his signature warehouse suits. With his large frame, they never fit right, and somebody had given him the bad advice of using a red bandana as a pocket handkerchief. He could have been any detective written out of any 1980s TV cop show.

Chief Terwig annoyed me—lots—but he never surprised me. I suspected good-cop Terwig, bogged down in the politics of a high-level position, constantly exposed to powerful favors, would someday be taken over by bad-cop Terwig. On the other hand, I had no evidence to support that suspicion. I had trusted him with important knowledge that I didn't think the feds should know about, and I hoped this wasn't karmic payback for trusting anyone but Charles Joseph Komensky.

The second person through the door didn't make my heart beat any easier. Judge Burmeister never dressed the part anymore. He'd been retired from the bench for more years than I'd been a CPD detective before chucking it for the suburbs, but he still did part-time court gigs and had a lot of influence. That day, he looked like somebody had dragged him right out of the cab of a locomotive. (He was actually a federally certified railway engineer—long story.) The look on his face said he'd rather be somewhere else. Better than Terwig, whose face I couldn't read at all.

Third in line: My old friend Georgio Luchesse. Nothing about his presence, other than the fact that he wasn't in handcuffs, boded well. His trim leather jacket didn't show the usual gun bulge. A bad sign.

Terwig sat behind the desk, and the other two pulled up a couple of side chairs. The chief grunted and motioned for Georgio to shut the door before he sat. I don't know why. With all the glass on both sides, a fishbowl would have been more private.

Sitting in front of Terwig like that, I raised my cuffed hands to suggest that it would be nice to get them off. Terwig just shrugged as if to say, "That depends." Then we sat for a couple minutes looking at each other like a bunch of bulls deciding who was going to make the first move on the cow.

Finally, Terwig sighed. With a ham-handed fist, he picked up a brand new lead pencil from the desk and then smashed it down so hard on the desktop that it shattered and sent the eraser end bouncing off onto the windowsill. "Komensky? You know I've given you a lot of latitude in the past." He paused, and if expecting an answer.

"Uh . . . Thank you?"

"No thanks necessary. A lotta times you deserved it. Like the other day when you gave me this video. I figured you deserved it with your girl getting killed in custody. I thought maybe you'd return the favor and keep me filled in on your investigation.

"And then!" His volume knob turned way up. "I find out that you and a wanted, international fugitive are icing out a federal agent!"

At this, Georgio squinted and turned his eyes toward the judge. When I looked at the judge, he just looked right back, stone-faced. Since the time a year or so before, when

I'd found out the judge didn't fit on the pedestal I put him on, it had been impossible for me to completely trust him. He claimed more than once that he did things for my own good, except that his version of my good and mine were running down different sides of the highway. Since Terwig was still waiting for my response, I said, "I expected to tell you before you found out from Judas."

Terwig exploded. "I don't care what your juvenile problem is with Judge Burmeister, Charlie. But you got no call to Judas him. He and the wiseguy have done a lot of good for the community and the department."

Once more I held up my cuffed wrists, then extended them palms out toward Terwig. I hoped he'd take it as a gesture of supplication, but couldn't help adding, "You're tying my hands the same way DHS did with Linda." Terwig reached into a shirt pocket, pulled out a little silver key, and tossed it onto the desk so that it stopped in front of me, just before falling off the edge. I readily undid the cuffs. "That woman you just threw in the hole is Linda's sister."

"Big revelation!" Terwig said, dripping with sarcasm. "I never would have guessed. Except I didn't get my detective stripes yesterday!"

The time for me to beg had come. "Please! Chief! Before you let somebody from Homeland interrogate her, take a swab. Langhoeffer, Henry, and Gloria nee Asturias. Died in Venezuela in 1979. Two kids, girls. Linda and Paula. They've got to have relatives somewhere. Get some DNA. Don't do to her sister what DHS did to Linda," I pleaded.

"Look, Charlie." Terwig glared at me. "I have no intention of becoming a shit-faced federal asshole, so don't make me tell you twice. We'll do the swabs. But you've got to give me something. The feds have agreed to let me get it from you, but I've got 48 hours to put it all together and hand it to them all wrapped up like a package of shit from the dog park.

"Burmeister did the right thing. If he hadn't gotten me involved, you'd be as disappeared as a black spot in a pile of coal. And Georgio did you a favor by telling me what he knows. It's not a good thing when somebody goes down a rabbit hole in Illinois and winds up in Minnesota.

"And then there's the Venezuelan Special Consul."

"What?" I yelled, springing up from the chair as though it had been electrified. "What Consul?"

"Don't look now," Terwig said, nodding and looking behind me. "Consul Villafuego has extradition papers for some woman named Paula San Cristobal. Looks a lot like the sister must have looked back in 1979. He's in the office across the hall." Terwig shoved several pages of official looking documents at me across the desk. "And sit the hell down."

For all of the Spanish parts I could read or the English parts I could understand, the papers could have been requesting that Bugs Bunny be sold to Azerbaijan. The ribbons and seals and strange stamps on it could have been distractions from the sheer fraudulence of the pages. I gave them a good once-over anyway, then said to Terwig, "Listen, Chief. I'm not an expert on foreign extradition, but I can tell you one important thing. Nobody but my main suspect in the murder of Marco Cajo would even think to use the last name of San Cristobal."

"And that suspect would be?" Terwig wasn't going to let it go.

"Someone with the same last name. Someone who has enough power and connections to summon a convincing Special Consul."

"This day just keeps getting better." Terwig sighed and shook his head. "I've got orders from DHS to let this Villafuego guy sit in with us when you go over your investigation."

The judge cut in. "I think I can help." He already had his smartphone out and punched up a contact. "I need a favor," he said into the phone when somebody answered. Five minutes later, Terwig had an email from Department of State with a document, signed by no less than the first undersecretary, ordering Terwig to hold Paula San Cristobal, a Venezuelan National, for 48 hours pending a review by State for any "abiding national interest" in granting her asylum. It was nice to have connected friends.

"You've still got to detain this fake consul," I pointed out. "Or he goes right back to his bosses and tells them we're on to him."

"Follow my lead," said Terwig, as he got up.

We did in fact follow him across the hall. I wouldn't have imagined that Terwig could be as cordial as he was in politely asking the consul to accompany us to another room for our meeting. Then he took us all down the hall, where he unlocked the door to a room that could have been a meeting room. Terwig bowed and said, "My distinct pleasure to have the honorable consul meet with us today." I watched the fake consul, and he was eating it up. "Oh, but before we go in. I'm going to have to ask everyone to check your cell phones at the door. We have a very delicate bit of information to discuss, and I don't want any interruptions or leaks."

Terwig pulled out his phone and we all did the same. The consul, somewhat reluctantly, handed Terwig his phone first. "After you. I'll just have my aide hold onto these."

The moment Villafuego had both feet across the threshold, Terwig have him a quick shove from behind and slammed the door to the supermax interrogation room shut behind him. It took a second, but when the consul realized he'd been bamboozled, he started a ruckus to wake the dead. "Hey! Senór? Senór! What are you doing? You cannot do this!" All the time pushing and knocking and banging.

"I've had suspects keep that up for ten, twelve hours like that," said Terwig matter-of-factly. "But they didn't get back out."

CHAPTER SIXTEEN

The deal was simple, even though the rest of the meeting with Terwig, Georgio, the judge and me lasted for several hours. Terwig needed a reason to resist compliance with the federal orders, and I could give him only part of it. What I had was an anecdotal report from a group of supposed Catholic militia that a respected clergyman was actually a child molester, murderer and rapist, and conspired with others to spread this criminal activity on an international basis. Even Paula's testimony wouldn't help. The rape of the Langhoeffer girls had occurred many years ago in another country. Even if it could be shown that someone had faked their death, it would take days, if not months, to mount a cooperative investigation in Venezuela—not the most cooperative of governments—to substantiate the claim.

Terwig would take no part in any plans to lure San Cristobal out of hiding, particularly to a sex den, unless San Cristobal committed a crime. The most he could do if the Black Bishop was caught with his pants down would be to arrest him on DC charges, and that wouldn't be enough to hold an influential foreign national overnight.

I got a nice pat on the back for the single most important clue, in Terwig's opinion, and that was the video showing the bombing of the museum to be a drone attack. When the feds connected that with the assault by drone in Beth's flat, and in the subway, then all hell would break loose under my feet. Terwig planned to comply with the 48 hours, unless I could come up with a better idea.

As with any good detective, Terwig's gut was telling him that my narrative was as true as it could get, given the missing hard evidence, and he started to go over it in his mind just in case he'd overlooked anything. "As far as I can tell," Terwig started, "the feds haven't been able to determine who was operating the drones that went after you. The signals were bounced through dozens of cell towers."

This surprised me. "Do you have your own network people on it?"

"So far, they confirm it. It's going to be a long slog to find the source."

I looked first at Judge Burmeister and then at Georgio, who appeared to be dozing. "That gives me an idea. I didn't consider it before, but now it makes perfect sense."

"What?" Terwig tensed up, as he always did when I caught something he'd missed. I never knew why. It wasn't like I was after his job or something.

"So far, I've assumed that the Montesans suffered a raid of their armory and the drones were stolen. But what if we assume that no drones, or any other armaments for that matter, were stolen."

Without appearing to wake up, Georgio answered, "Then the damn Catholic Church blew up Dr. Cajo!"

Terwig now. "Or the Templars did." After thinking a few seconds, a scowl crossed his face. "But how do we use that?"

"Take a look at what we do have evidence for, and tell me what's not right." I knew none of them would spot it, but I gave them a few seconds. "The odd couple of Eddie Figg and Danita Cambrero. She's educated, a looker, had access to everything the victim heard and did during his last months, and turned down Eddie's advances publicly. Eddie's a loser wannabe cop who didn't even know when to keep his gun holstered. But we've got instant messages between the two since the murders. Nothing incriminating, but you've got to ask yourself why. And then there's my cell phone photo of the two of them in more than intimate circumstances at Beth's party. There's got to be something."

"So what's your plan?" Terwig asked with interest.

"This is an unsolved murder on the books of your department, right?"

"Don't remind me."

"Can you rule out Figg or Cambrero as persons of interest?"

"Well." Terwig hesitated. "We don't think they were flying any drones."

"Forget the drones for a minute," I said, shaking my head. "Get a search warrant for Cambrero's apartment, and make it as broad as the judge will go for. Let me come with your team, and don't alert the feds. I've got a feeling we'll get some answers."

We had failed to notice, but sometime during our meeting, Villafuego's banging and yelling had stopped. As we came down the hall, confident in what we were going to do and say when the warrant was served, Terwig was the first to notice the open door. The supermax had been breached, and nobody had heard it or could say when or how it happened. The absence of forced entry suggested an inside job, or was it just an enemy who had soldiers in all the right places? Terwig thought of Paula a half second after I did. A quick cell call revealed that she, too, had left her room.

A quick look at the security cameras for HQ found an unaccompanied Villafuego getting into a black sedan that just drove up as he strolled out the front door. Neither the plates nor the driver could be imaged. No images could be retrieved from the interrogation rooms or from the cameras in the immediate corridors. The digital information from both rooms and corridors, up to the moment the doors stood ajar, had been written over, right on the police server, with a precision that made Terwig blanch. There had been no visualization of Paula's escape. Was that intentional? If not an inside job, then a job done by someone with one hell of a remote control. Were they telling us—telling me—that we had no hope of controlling this situation?

The chief barked some explicit, profanity-enhanced orders that heads would not only roll but also get booted across the city like so many soccer balls. He shot me the evil eye, an eye that told me I'd better be right about this, and we all shook hands and went about the business of sleeping for what was left of the night. Terwig would call us when the warrant was ready. I knew I wouldn't sleep or rest.

Paula on the run. Did Villafuego have her? Did San Cristobal have both of them? The scenarios ran over and over like a bad series of internet videos without benefit of commercial interruption during the few hours I tried to sleep on Georgio's couch. What happened if you unwrapped the toy in the pink wrapper? Every door in every office in HQ flew open at the same time, and a thousand Villafuegos and another thousand Paula Langhoeffers walked out and faded down the blackness of a mile-long hallway. My mind had traded Linda nightmares for Paula nightmares.

When the phone on the coffee table woke me up, the intense headache of the day before had returned. I knew I should get it checked out, but I didn't want to spend another night in a hospital while things went so far south that wild penguins got run down.

I'd never been to Georgio's apartment before that day; in fact, I didn't recall ever having been invited. I suppose this time maybe the reformed gangster had no choice. The second-floor flat in an old neighborhood of two- and three-flat brick buildings of 1920s vintage seemed serviceable, but I'd expected more. I guess Georgio spent more time keeping up mob appearances with flashy clothes and accessories than with lavish parties. With a mixed bag of furniture straight out of eBay and Costco, the most defining feature of décor was a full-sized gun safe standing along the free wall of the dining room.

Georgio grabbed his cellphone and looked at the caller ID. "Luchesse," he answered. The caller must have been short and to the point, because Georgio dismissed the call in two seconds and said to me, "Come on, sleeping beauty, the warrant is on." He withdrew what looked like a Smith and Wesson .44 Magnum from the safe, pocketed a box of ammo, closed the door and spun the dial. This gave me just enough time to zip up my pants and grab my jacket before he was out the door and on his way down the stairs.

When we got to the high rise and the mobile crime unit was parked in the circle drive, I got a bad feeling about the whole operation. More than one police vehicle was marked with a supervisor's number, and at least two officers were checking IDs at the revolving doors. Inside the lobby, where I had rushed through in an effort to draw the drone away from Beth's apartment not long before, the chief and Judge Burmeister huddled with a suit who must have been an assistant DA and another who could have been internal affairs. Because of the crowd, we stayed to one side and waited for the judge and the chief to notice us, which they did and finally separated themselves and walked over.

Never one to spare a drop of emotional salve, Terwig looked me up and down and said, "We've got a body."

I don't know what came over me, but the recalled trauma of Linda's arrest and the news of her death while I was helpless in a hospital bed overwhelmed me like the smell of piss and beer from the open door of a cheap tavern on a hot afternoon. "Oh, no! Not Paula, too?" I staggered a bit and felt Georgio's big hands under my armpits and dragging me to one of the lounges. Someone brought me a bottle of fancy water and made me drink. The stuff tasted like rancid cooking oil, so naturally I choked on it and it just made things worse. Not only was my headache almost unbearable, but I was having trouble focusing again.

Knowing when to push on and when to just shut up and take your lumps was not a part of police academy when I attended it, so I stood up and directed, "Let's go take a look at the stiff."

"Charlie! It's not Linda's sister," Georgio said, trying to calm me down. "It's the assistant. Cambrero."

I looked from Georgio's face to Burmeister's, and then to Terwig, who was snickering a little. "Like I said. Let's go look at the stiff."

The breakfast I hadn't had took a shot at coming up anyway, and I had to hold hard onto the railing in the elevator on the way up. Breakfast on the shoes or not, I wasn't going to miss this chance to stay on the ground floor of what was yet another investigation that would lead to one of the same two suspects. Either San Cristobal had killed Cajo, or the Templars had. One or the other had killed Linda. And one or the other maybe planned the same fate for Linda's sister. I wasn't going to be the sharpest cutlery in the drawer, but this was for Linda.

One thing about stiffs; they never look like themselves. But this was Cambrero all right. The AME had left the body in situ, not even a cover, because of all the forensic work that would have to be done. Sprawled in the middle of her living room, a room that approximated the same layout as Beth Pea's place, Cambrero lay on her back, but turned slightly to her right. Her left leg bent at the knee and her left heel almost touched her buttocks. Her right arm lay straight out in front of her face, which was also turned to her left. Her left arm just languished over and behind her back. And she was just as totally naked as when I had seen her at the sex party. Except this dead, naked girl was far from titillating, because each and every one of the strange tattoos I had seen the night before was cut out of her dead flesh, leaving only brownish red strips about two inches long and half an inch wide.

I could see a large, bloody wound just under her sternum; the kind of wound that would be made by a surprise attack by someone you trusted using an extremely lethal blade, like a stiletto or a bayonet. The blow would have had to have been delivered by someone with close combat training or experience, someone who knew how to end a life in one of the most personal ways possible.

The AME kneeled on one knee and stooped over her, looking intently at her face. "Was she sexually assaulted?" I asked, already knowing the answer.

"Sexually active? Yeah, but I don't think it's rape. This one was a fuckin' rabbit."

"What do you see there?" I realized that something wasn't right with her face.

"Broken nose and two teeth fractured. She liked it rough."

"It's not a lover," I said. "I think she's been staged like this. But enjoy yourself."

I turned to Terwig, who was standing aside, reluctant to interfere in a case that rightfully belonged to one of his detectives. "I know what you're thinking," he said before I spoke. "We've already got a BOLO out on Eddie Figg. I had the judge here call Figg's attorney."

"Can't you see this isn't the work of some two-bit security guard?"

"No, I can't. Frankly, Komensky, I don't know what to think. Maybe you killed her."

"You're joking."

"If I didn't know you better, I wouldn't be. But maybe Figg didn't get what he wanted from her last night. Or maybe he did. Maybe there's a direct line from Beth Pea's door to this one. Sex, or the withholding of it, is a powerful motive for murder."

I just shook my head and walked away. It didn't add up. If Figg wanted the numbers and letters on her skin, he probably could have photographed them just like I did the night before. Why would he want to cut them out of her? No. This was somebody sending a message. Somebody who knew that the numbers were connected to something, and once they were within his grasp, knew also that they weren't going to be enough. The murderer was taunting us, taunting me.

With the burner phone, the same one I had from last night when I took the pics of Danita Cambrero's naked torso, I quickly called my hacker friend Ops. The message center said, "Universal Digital Access is accepting only text messages at this time," and then gave a text address. That frustrated me, because I was about as good at entering text with my thumbs as I was at holding salad tongs with my toes. That, and my vision was still fading in and out. I managed to tell him what I needed and email him the Cambrero pics from the night before.

Terwig saw me and came over with a mischievous look on his face. "Tick, tock!"

"You got a clock up your ass, Chief?"

He frowned. "You know the good news is we'll have a broader search warrant in about twenty minutes. But you probably should be making plans to get out of town. I'm still going to talk to the feds on schedule."

"That still gives me about thirty-six hours," I observed. "And I think I'm going to beat the clock."

"Suit yourself, Komensky. But I'm still not getting on the San Cristobal slash Templar wagon unless something concrete turns up. I guess you an' Goombah are gonna be on your owns."

CHAPTER SEVENTEEN

O f course, Terwig wasn't kidding. He seldom kidded about anything, but in this case he also issued an order so nobody in the department would even think of taking an off-duty swing past the Humboldt Park site of what was to be our confrontation with San Cristobal. To make matters worse, Georgio put out feelers to every mob crew he knew, and they all came back negative. Even a Russian crew was too superstitious to consider the possibility of having to kill a priest, faux or not.

I convinced Georgio that I needed to get home, shower and shave, and get a change of clothes. This time, home would be Linda's place; something I'd dreaded since she'd been killed. But we weren't going to make it. We'd picked up the other laptop from my office, and were on our way from there to Linda's when I suddenly woke up laying on the couch in Dr. Sparks' office with a crick in my neck and an IV in my arm. The clock on the wall showed it was after four. I'd lost half the day.

"Doc Sparks used the doggie-ray on you," said Georgio. Seated on a chair next to me, he didn't look up from his year-old magazine. "You got a brain thingy that might kill you."

I sat up with difficulty. "A brain thingy?"

"A lesion. You got a lesion. And you're dehydrated. That's why the drip."

It turned out that I'd just gone to sleep in Georgio's car, and he couldn't wake me up. At least he had the good sense not to take me to MacNeal Hospital. "Any news on Paula?"

"Nobody's seen or heard from her, and the cops ain't talkin'. And no, you didn't get any texts from Ops, either. Only good news is we still got thirty hours and one of my boys has Eddie Figg in a safe house on Karlov. Turns out Eddie knew one of the sharks and was trying to borrow enough money to get out of town."

"Has he said anything?"

"Lotta fowl mouth bullshit. But the guys'll soften him up. 'Less you want the honor." He grinned.

"Let's go!" I said eagerly.

"Not until you finish that bag o' blood sugar; an' you know I mean it."

He did, so it was about 7:00 p.m. before we got to the safe house, a turn-of-the-twentieth, frame two-story still covered with the kind of 50s style, grey asphalt siding that was supposed to look like flagstone. By that time, Georgio's "guys," a couple of goons who had no idea that Georgio worked with the police or why Figg was there, had Figg sautéed in butter and simmering like bell peppers for Italian beef, getting softer and more transparent by the minute. He still wore his security uniform pants and jacket, though the latter was open, dirty and torn at the neck. They had him duct taped to a radiator in all the right places, and that was okay with me.

"Who are you?" Figg looked at me defiantly, and then started to think he recognized me. "Hey! I seen you before."

I thought I'd better deprive him of that idea as fast as possible, so I changed the subject. "Nice of you to come out and visit us without your lawyer."

"Fuck you!" One of the guys stepped in and put the back of a smoked-ham-sized hand across his chops. He groaned and spit out some blood. "I paid that other loan back. I swear it," he blubbered, his bruised lips getting thicker by the second.

"Errrrrk! Wrong answer!"

As Georgio's guy hovered, Figg thought a bit, and then said, "She was dead when I got there. I swear it."

"You do a lot of swearing for a sworn officer," I pointed out. "But that's strike two."

Ham Hand moved a little closer. "Okay! Okay! Just tell Hulk to back off."

I nodded to the guy and he stepped back into a corner while Georgio stood behind me. "You took something from Cajo before the explosion, didn't you?"

"No. I didn't. I sw . . . Shit!"

"Do I have to have the brick crapper come back over here and loosen up your memory and maybe your bowels a little more?"

"NO! I mean. I didn't take anything, but I was supposed to. I was supposed to try to get something from Cajo's safe, but I didn't get it."

"You were supposed to?"

"Yeah."

"For who?"

"That tattooed little South American slut."

"Danita Cambrero?"

"Yeah. Danita. I was supposed to look for an opportunity to get some art facts out of the safe."

"You mean artifacts?"

"Whatever. When I saw Cajo run into the building alone, I thought I'd just put a gun butt upside his head and find the combination. When I got inside the suite, there was Cajo in front of the safe trying to close it. Like he was trying to protect something from me. I bashed him with my service piece and shoved him aside. He was groaning and dazed. I opened that damn safe. And you'll never guess what I found." He paused for dramatic effect. "Nothing! That's what. Zip!

"I was on my way back out into the hall when the whole place went up in flames. I turned around and there was Lazy Johnson comin' out of the smoke with a gun in his hands. I thought to myself that he took the arty facts an' was workin' for someone else, so I plugged 'im. But no art facts. Then I grew this story that I gave the cops, 'an here we are. Satisfied?"

It sounded plausible, but, if true, where the hell was the evidence that Cajo had on San Cristobal? "What did Cambrero say when you told her there was nothing in there?"

After thinking for a little too long for my taste, Figg answered, "She said she'd have her boss take care of it, and me, if I was lying to her."

"Her boss? Did she say who?"

"Just that there wouldn't be anywhere I could hide if I was screwing with her and him."

I asked Georgio to keep him at the house for a few days until everything got sorted out, and then strongly suggested to Figg that he step up and tell the truth when he had the next chance. "We have friends who can protect you in prison," I noted. "But outside, I think Cambrero might be right."

We got out of the tarpaper mansion on Karlov about half past ten. I couldn't help but feel the clock ticking down without any hope of getting a break in the case. In twenty-four hours, we'd have to confront San Cristobal. And the choices at our disposal weren't pretty.

The Templars wanted the monster figuratively crucified, and I didn't blame them. The church needed the world to know that it had excised the main cancer from inside, and they needed the opportunity to learn as much about his filthy network of molesters and murderers as possible. They needed to keep cutting until all the cancer was cut out. To do that, they needed the evidence that seemed then to have vanished into thin air.

Without it, our only script for the party was to effectively assassinate San Cristobal, which would make him a martyr and probably strengthen his dark followers and make them more difficult for the church to root out. Without putting it too strongly, I thought, killing San Cristobal, the Black Bishop, could just possibly cause the fall of the Catholic Church.

Paula Langhoeffer remained a sidebar. She'd vanished along with Villafuego, who appeared to have more attachments than a food processor when it came to the Black Bishop. Did that mean she was with him? Or against him? I had no way of knowing.

Fittingly, that night, I convinced myself that I had sufficiently evaded San Cristobal's surveillance techniques; as long as a sweep of the neighborhood showed up nothing out of the ordinary, I could spend my first night at Linda's since her arrest—and since her death. It turned out I was right, but that didn't make the night any more pleasant. And, as far as choosing a place with more psychological triggers than an Alfred Hitchcock movie, I hit the stupid moves lottery.

The bedroom reminded me of making love to Linda. The shower reminded me of it. The living room in front of the TV reminded me of it. The washer-dryer in the basement didn't, but it reminded me of doing laundry which reminded me of the time we undressed down there and just threw in our clothes, which reminded me . . . oh, you get the picture. Then there were the boatload of what-ifs. What if I had smuggled her out the back when the feds came calling? What if we had just shot our way out? What if I had gotten myself arrested and transported with her? How could I have done that? It seemed pretty clear that she would have still been a target of the Black Bishop whether or not we had met, but what if she had just told me about her past? Could we have done anything before things got out of hand?

At a half past one, with a full moon lighting up a clear, late-spring sky that you would swear still held the glow of a solstice sun circling far in the north, I went out and sat on Linda's front porch. We'd made love there, too. The chirp of crickets hadn't yet given way to the locusts that would buzz all summer once the Fourth of July was past, and no amount of my trying to think of anything else but Linda was going to give way to a decent night's sleep. I tried to will a break in the case. Ops might call. Or one of Morgan's men might wrap a cloth filled with chloroform around my face and take me to another covert base. Terwig might have a change of heart. What did I have? Less than twenty hours then.

The drugs that Doc Sparks had given me were wearing off, and I admit that I didn't take his advice and drink a lot of water, either. So, I did the next best thing and raided Linda's pantry, found a full bottle of Ten High—ugh—and treated the returning headache with some proof.

Luchesse found me passed out on the front porch at eight in the morning. The Thursday traffic had already started to jam up on Riverside Drive, and the railroad that crossed the drive at grade a half mile away was doing its best to contribute to the chaos. If I'd been half my regular self, I would have taken a walk down to the crossing to watch some locomotives pass. As I came out of the stupor, I realized the weather had turned cloudy, and it looked like it might drizzle even though the temperature was going to hold at warm. It wouldn't be Northeastern Illinois if we didn't get to ninety degrees and ninety percent humid before the middle of June.

My head gave me another twinge as I tried to focus on Georgio. "Unngh!" I groaned.

"Good morning to you, too, asshole," he responded. "Who told you it was a good idea to drink that rotgut on top of vet medicine? We've got work to do today, if we're going to track down that evidence before ten tonight."

It was at that moment I realized that the green light was blinking on my phone and Ops had been trying to reach me since about four. I forgot about the headache and thumbed up the hacker. The information he had to impart was simple, though he had to go through a convoluted series of explanations about how he figured it out. I didn't need to know that unless I was going to go into breaking into government databases myself, and I wasn't.

The essence of it seemed too slick to be the product of Cambrero's brain alone. The six tattoos corresponded to the digital network routing for HD-only control signals. In the right order, the last of them went straight to the digital receiver that the feds had found on the drone from the subway. Though it wasn't concrete proof, it meant she could be the pilot of one or both drones. So if Commander Morgan's story was true, San Cristobal had been controlling Cambrero. I didn't forget that Morgan's story could be fabricated. After all, not like they would produce receipts, but the drones supposedly belonged to the Templars.

Being the thorough hacker that he was, however, Ops had also looked for any other meanings for the multi-character passwords, and found those meanings in the access codes for several online "cloud" servers. "I can't tell you exactly where these servers are located," he apologized. "That's why they call it the cloud. But I can tell you that, in the same order, each of those passwords leads to a cloud file, which has an address to another cloud file that needs the next password, etc., until you get to the last file, that required a password we don't have."

"Did you check all the pics I took."

"Buddy, I blew them up on my eighty-inch Samsung and there weren't any other tats on that body. And it was an interesting body."

I chuckled. "I bet you did."

"Hey!" Ops exclaimed. "I don't usually get to look at pics from a sex party and get paid for it. About that."

"You'll get your money when the client pays me. Like we arranged." Georgio just stood over me and grinned, because I had a bit of a rep with some of the informants I used. Not a few had gone to the organization to enquire about muscle to make me pay my bills. "Thanks, Ops. We'll square up soon. I promise." I ended the call and turned to Georgio, "So. Any ideas?"

"You first."

"I think the final password was supposed to be in the safe, and it got incinerated."

"You're the dick."

I shrugged. "If that's true, then the evidence on Cristobal is somewhere floating around in cyberspace. Without the password, he's been safe all along; and all this was for nothing." Taking my phone back out of my pocket, I hit last call. When Ops picked it up, I asked, "Can you hack it?"

I waited through a long pause. "It's a two-fifty-six bit encrypted piece of work. It'll take hours!"

"Okay, okay! Georgio here says he'll work me over himself if I don't pay you a bonus."

Another pause. "I'm gonna need five figures."

"Buddy, you do this? I'll buy you five Mustang GTs." I saw Georgio wince as I said it. "Maybe just one."

"I'll see what I can do." And the call dropped.

I looked at Georgio and he looked back, neither of us believing that the whole caper could be for nothing. Three dead, maybe four. "Are you cryin'?" he asked.

"My headache is makin' my eyes water."

CHAPTER EIGHTEEN

Sometimes, I wondered why I spent all those years making contacts and fleshing out connections in the criminal underworld. Other times, like that day, I felt like the gods of vice, extortion, torture and murder had choked up a rare favor in return for my looking the other way to protect my informants. We found an empty house we could use, across the street and on the same block as the sex mistress' townhouse in Humboldt Park.

One of the many scams run by the Italian mob in Chicago was the halfway house. The mob had petty con men out in every neighborhood running one or more of these spigots of liquid cash direct from the government. The mob backed the purchase of a dilapidated house that would be set up to accommodate as many of societies unfortunates as building codes could be bribed to allow. The petty con had to pay back the mob loan at probably six times the going rate for a regular mortgage, plus something off the top. But what a top! The unfortunates—mentally ill, disabled, recently prison-released, addicted, alcoholic, whatever—depended on what government body happened to be doling out the big money at the particular time. All the operator of the halfway had to do was provide low-priced meals and counseling, both also to be purchased from the mob, and the rest was gravy. The thought of a wiseguy having a PhD in psychology made me chuckle. More than likely, an actual psychologist would be blackmailed or extorted to provide free service. In Georgio's world, skeletons lurking in closets came equipped with cash drawers.

Our spot across from the sex mistress had been slated to house six former inmates on their way to recidivism, but Georgio had coopted it with a promise of a break from certain authorities if the con ever got caught. On our way over there, we picked up three more burner phones, a cheap digital camera, six dozen donuts, a fistful of magazines, and a case of thirty-two cans of cola. We also made one more stop at the vet's and secured three syringes full of animal tranquilizers. Once inside the empty house, Georgio went back out to a Frugal Freddy and bought a couple of cheap aluminum folding chairs and a tasteless sports jacket in my size. He said it would help me put over my disguise as a sex pervert. "Right now, you look like a pervert that's also a detective," he said derisively. "It's all about image."

"Hey! We didn't have any trouble fitting in the other night."

"That's 'cause the hot number you were with made it believable. Here you gotta look like you wanna fondle grade-schoolers."

Since we didn't expect any action at Mistress Tally's— that's what she was called—until after seven at the earliest, we had time to go over the plan. Still with no backup, we agreed that we would keep the place under surveillance until the Black Bishop showed up. All I had were the pics on the laptop that Morgan had emailed to me, but I was confident we would recognize him. Then I would go in as a referral from our informant at Mistress Beth's—my name would be Roman Hand—while Georgio would take up a position outside the townhouse. With any luck, I could lure Cristobal out into the alley with a promise of some young flesh. Like the wiseguys say, bada-boom, bada-bing, we would have an unconscious prick tied up in our halfway house until we could figure out what to do with him. We had to hope all this would happen before the feds' artificial deadline. I had all the confidence in the world that Terwig would keep his promises, but none that the feds wouldn't pressure him to cough up the whole case sooner than expected. I had no confidence that we would find the missing evidence against San Cristobal somewhere up there in the cloud before the deadline passed.

Georgio needed to stay the dirtiest shade of white that he could, for the sake of the work he did with Judge Burmeister, so if the deadline passed without evidence, I would take San Cristobal directly to the feds and hope for the best. Even time in the Bridewell seemed better than leaving the Black Bishop on the street without even a chance of the feds interrogating him about his latest three murders. Maybe the headache and the fatigue were clouding my judgment, but, without telling Georgio, I had decided that I wouldn't resist any temptation to just shoot San Cristobal, and damn the consequences.

Once we had gone over the plan a couple of times, and Georgio had assured me that he could administer an incapacitating dose of the horse tranks without alerting the neighborhood, we settled in on the third floor and I picked up a set of binoculars to survey the block. Tally's was the east end of four connected three-story townhouses probably built by some contractor during the recent recession after demolishing a few foreclosures among the nearly hundred-year-old three-flats in the neighborhood. East of Tally's was an empty lot, maybe where the contractor came up against failure. The other three townhouses in the group appeared to be occupied, although the two closest to Tally's were the most obviously occupied, with spring garden window boxes and front door decorations. The western unit seemed a little drab, and the shades were pulled. Perhaps it wasn't occupied, or the tenant just didn't enjoy the block-party lifestyle. As I would have expected from somebody who didn't want to call too much attention to herself, Tally's unit ran the middle line between looking lived-in and looking inviting.

There wasn't anything to do but the peculiar kind of fried-food gluttony and visual self-gratification practiced by cops on a stakeout.

We took turns at the magazines, but a fistful wasn't enough. While Georgio read, I watched Tally's, and vice versa. About six thirty, while I was catching my third glimpse of *SkInput Magazine*'s ten sexiest bodies in Hollywood, a catering truck pulled up at Tally's and delivered booze, cheap snack food, and enough throw-away plates and cutlery for about forty people. In contrast to Beth's shindig, no spandex-clad servers stayed behind with the order. I guessed the really deep dregs of perversion needed sustenance but no atmosphere.

Georgio's turn at the binoculars had another twenty minutes to go, so I picked up a copy of *Hollow Point*, and, in desperation, started reading some of the advertising. Most of it was for firearms and ammo, and some was for accessories like body armor, holsters, fancy gear, you name it. On page twenty-three, I ran across an ad from a security company for the Aggressor 322, a floor- or wall-safe system. It hit me that the safe in Cajo's suite at the museum had been an Aggressor model, but I didn't recall the number. "The Aggressor's unique digital serial number," said the ad, "is an electronic registration number that provides an absolutely unique identity which can be determined with a cellphone app keyed with the recorded combination for the safe. The serial number is a patented, proprietary 256-bit ROM in a secure device whose specifications are known only to the safe manufacturer. This serial number also includes an 8-bit CRC, and an 8-bit Family Code. Data is transferred serially over an encrypted 802.11g, b, c connection initiated by the app and powered by a lithium ion battery embedded in the safe wall (estimated to last for the lifetime of the safe.) No other power source needs to be attached to the safe." I also didn't remember anything about getting a unique serial number, other than the brass plate on the front, in the police report.

Suddenly Georgio said, "Get your dancin' shoes on, I got guests arriving."

"Start the video, I've got to send Ops a quick message," I ordered.

"Hey! Who was your bitch on the last stakeout?"

"Please?" I begged. "I think I've got an idea."

"Okay, Idea Man. Camera started."

It looked like I wouldn't have time for a casual conversation with Ops about the merits of my idea, so I emailed him the magazine's online issue number and page and the advertiser code with the text:

isn't this like what you want for pword? can you locate museum safe and decrypt or contact/hack manufacturer? try for final pword for cloud file & let me kno asap. if near 10 also let CPD kno.

And I gave him the direct line to Terwig's cellphone.

I knew it was a longshot, but Ops was a pretty smart guy. In the meantime, we surveyed and counted everyone who came to the front door. With no backup, I had to be satisfied that Tally would need to screen guests, so only one entrance would be in use. Again in contrast to Beth's party, the guests' wardrobe, class, and apparent intelligence level screamed "loser" louder than the graduation list at a community college. Seven o'clock passed, and then eight. As time went by and the sun started to set, a few well-dressed people, maybe those who had gone out to a before-kinky-sex dinner—maybe oysters and chocolate-dipped strawberries—straggled in.

Nothing came from Ops, and nothing from the judge, who would have told us if Chief Terwig had anything new. I resisted the urge to call Ops again. Any interruption might just mess up his concentration enough to destroy our chances. Only a little more than an hour remained before Terwig would have to dump the case in the laps of every federal agency that the Venezuelan government might have complained to by then.

At ten to nine, a solitary, walking figure dressed in black slacks, a black shirt, and a cleric's collar turned the corner from Homan and strolled east on Crystal. Even though the sun had set and twilight had set in, I could see from the shape of the walker's head that he was the Black Bishop. Upon walking up to Tally's door and saying the right things to whoever answered—that we couldn't see—San Cristobal was admitted to what I hoped would be the last den of perversion he'd ever see.

"You're up!" Georgio said as he put away the camera. "Give me fifteen minutes to get into position in the alley, and we're good to go. Turn on the voice recorder on your phone, keep it in your pants, and we'll be okay."

Tally, an unexpectedly cute black woman with smallish features and immense breasts, answered the door herself. She seemed to accept the information Henry had given me as entre, but balked at taking a fake platinum card as admission. Good thing I'd gotten Georgio to loan me a grand in cash at "company rates" before I left the halfway house. "Won' leave y'all much fuh tips," she said, looking me up and down. "Lessin yuh wants tuh tip me ovah a couple times." She followed up this comment with a lewd grin and a laugh that needed to be decontaminated.

The nice, tasteful, chic modern furniture in her home was what I would have expected for a young, successful businesswoman with enough money to live well. The empty parlor suggested that the party was upstairs, so I automatically went toward the single staircase. "Unh, unh!" she warned, and I turned with some surprise. "Straight tuh the back an' left. Use the green do'."

I expected to walk into a party room or lounge setup, but instead, beyond that green door, I saw nothing but a long hallway, punctuated only by oddly-spaced florescent lighting, that stretched maybe 150 feet straight ahead of me. My heart sank, and I could feel my blood pressure rise. The sex parties didn't even take place in Tally's unit, but apparently in the unit on the west end of the block of four. No wonder the exterior looked so drab and had all the shades pulled!

Instinctively, I turned to attempt a retreat. I somehow had to warn Georgio, and thereby our non-existent backup, should it ever decide to materialize, that I wouldn't be where he thought. But Tally stood right behind me, gave me a dirty look, and said, "If yo' havin' cold feet, yo' bettah leave now. I ain' comin' back answer no do' fo' no fuckah ain' got no balls AN' no money!"

In spite of the multiple double negatives, I got the picture and kept on walking. At the west end of the corridor, we made another left and entered the first floor of the west unit. Tally had industriously opened up most of the partitions, removed the kitchen, installed a wet bar in its place, and generally decorated the resulting large room in a faux Victorian style of soft, dark furniture, frilly accents, and very dimly lit wall sconces and a single chandelier—everything you would expect in a nineteenth century whorehouse. The smells of booze, lilac, and body heat filled the enclosed space. Somewhere in the unit, a stereo played elevator music, and an air conditioner worked to keep the late day heat out and eject the odors. It wasn't working.

Tally let me loose with an "Enjoy yo'self," and slowly blended into the décor. The party activities going on were just about what I would have expected after visiting Beth Pea's party, though the sex seemed a lot rougher and a lot more boisterous. I circulated a while, didn't see San Cristobal anywhere, and reached the stairs to the second floor, located about in the same place where they were in the floor plan of Tally's unit.

A tacky sign on the bannister had an arrow pointing up and said, "To Next Level," so I followed it, feeling a bit like Alice in wonderland and a bit like a tourist dropped into Dante's *Devine Comedy*.

The second floor indeed reached the next level of sexual gratification, with floggings, restraint, and other things I hoped I wouldn't ever feel the need be a part of. But it wasn't the time for judgment, preaching, driving the demons out, or any of those things one wants to do when the angel on your shoulder tells you to avert your eyes. I'd already been in there too long, and Georgio would be set up and waiting to administer the excising injection out in the alley.

The sign on the door to the third floor stairway had an arrow pointing up, but no words to describe the disturbing things one could expect to find above. With no trace of my quarry on the first two levels, and running out of time, I somewhat hesitantly opened the door.

Behind it, Eduardo San Cristobal descended the stairs with a smile on his face, his priestly garb making him look like he had just experienced a holy vision. He looked at me a little quizzically, but didn't appear to recognize me, and said, "Oh, I don't think a country boy like you is ready for heaven yet." His Spanish accent was not nearly as pronounced as I had expected.

As he descended and closed the door behind him, I put on my best shy, bashful voice, threw in a little stammer, and said, "I . . . I was looking . . . looking for you, Monsignor."

The monster reached out and put a hand on my shoulder, reminding me that I would have to burn the tacky jacket right after this was all over. Close up and real for the first time, he looked harmless, almost a Santa Claus, with a left cheek dimple and twinkling, dark eyes. A swirl of unusually yellow blonde hair that fell sideways as if styled that way didn't fit with his Spanish and native South American features. He smiled a jovial but shallow smile and said, "For me? Or for a priest? There are a couple of lovely nuns here that I think you would like."

"No sir." I kept my gaze down and whispered, "Harvey told me you wanted to meet some young people. You know."

I could almost feel the darkness overwhelm him as he responded, "Young people. Yes! The younger the better, if you know what I mean. Did you bring them with you?"

"They're out . . . out in my van. Around the side. Through the alley."

Big smile. "Well, then. Let's go out the back, onto the porch and go get them. I'm sure they'll love it upstairs."

"Got him," I thought, but I kept one hand in my pocket, grasping one of the three syringes I had taken with me just in case. If it came to it, there was always my .38 tucked firmly in my waistband above my left butt cheek. Georgio was sure to see us come out the back, even if he was three doors down.

We dodged a couple of legs that were protruding from under a coffee table and found a door that led to an open back porch. The night had become stifling with no wind, any trace of twilight had disappeared, and loud party music thrashed the air from a house across the alley and a few doors over. Even in the middle of the city, crickets were winning the battle to drown it out. A single bare bulb illuminated the well-constructed wooden porch. I started for the stairs when Cristobal said, "Hold it just a minute." I turned and saw him take my picture with a cell phone he'd pulled from a pocket on the way out. He seemed to have transmitted my picture somewhere, but I couldn't tell for sure. "You won't mind a few precautions," he stated flatly. I clutched the syringe even tighter and led the way down the back stairs, but I couldn't help noticing Cristobal hanging back, no longer quite as eager.

The door from the first floor opened suddenly outward, blocking my path as I came to the landing. A burly white man with a shaved head, also dressed as a priest emerged and closed the door, but continued blocking my path. How did I miss this guy on my way up? I let go of the syringe and prepared to go for my .38, when the lug made a quick move and got hold of my gun hand, taking it over against me and pinning me to the wall, where he frisked me and removed the syringe, my cell phone, and the .38. Then he put me in a choke hold and hustled me back up the stairs, following Cristobal, with my own gun pointed at what was left of my brains. How could I have let this happen, and where was Georgio?

We continued on up past the second floor landing and to the third floor, where Cristobal stood out on the porch making a cell call while Father Burly hustled me inside. Once he had me seated in a wooden chair and my hands secured behind me with a zip tie, he continued to stand over me with my gun muzzle behind my right ear. I had a chance to look around the room, although turning my head too far in either direction resulted in a painful prod behind my ear. The third floor had the same open format at the other two, only this level had been decorated into more of a dungeon-like appearance. Heavy brown blackout drapes hung over any windows and over other parts of the walls. The only light came from a candelabra type chandelier and cast foreboding shadows in every corner and in the folds of the drab drapery.

In front of me, on the wooden floor and secured with large lag bolts into the oak, sat a device like one I had seen in use at Beth's apartment. It looked like some kind of exercise equipment, and maybe could be used as such, but in practice it allowed the visionary practitioner of S & M to secure the submissive stretched out on his or her back with both arms pulled and tied down toward the floor and with legs spread wide open, knees bent backwards, and feet secured under the buttocks—a very uncomfortable and sexually vulnerable position for either sex. A chest of drawers in rough, brown wood stood on the wall opposite me. I imagined that all sorts of sexual devices resided there, but preferred to think about ways out.

Behind me and the chair, I guessed about three feet, a long railing separated the room from the stairway back to the second floor, which had not been partitioned off. I also guessed that the drop over the railing at the front end, where the stairs reached the door I'd tried to use earlier, at about twelve feet. I decided to wait, barring any sign of the cavalry, for an opportunity to jump over the railing and get the hell out.

We waited like that, me and Father Burly, for about twenty minutes. Georgio certainly would have tried to get help by then, but I also understood Terwig's position. Staying out of it made his life easier, he probably wouldn't even try to get a search warrant, and what was one more or less private detective in a city like Chicago? And I couldn't see Burmeister sticking his judge neck out on a warrant for just Georgio's testimony, no matter how valuable a CI he was. No. Unless Ops had come up with something, it was my game and their rules. Absolutely nothing in the investigation that Terwig would give the feds in just a few minutes would result in any charges against San Cristobal, but my ass, if it survived, would be a different story.

The porch door opening made Father Burly jump, my first indication that he could be less than composed in the face of a threat. He took the gun off me for just a fraction, but not long enough for me to make a move. San Cristobal led a third man, not dressed as a priest but wearing black slacks, shoes and a black tee under a black, leather shoulder holster, looking the part of a Colombian drug lord, through the door. The Colombian carried a large, black duffel, big enough to carry a lot of equipment, and dropped it noisily on the floor. A groan, a female groan, issued from it in response. As if he'd rehearsed the ritual, he drew his gun, a .480 Ruger Super Redhawk, pointed it at the duffel bag, and unzipped it. "Vaminos," he ordered.

A pair of female hands emerged straight up, followed in short by the rest of Paula Langhoeffer. I started to speak to her, but felt the muzzle of my .38 press harder behind my ear. Paula, still dressed in the black leathers, but barefoot, blinked and seemed to have trouble focusing, even in the dim light, and she appeared shaky and distressed. How long had they had her confined in that bag? What had they done to her?

San Cristobal gestured at the S & M machine, and a big grin broke on the Colombian's face. He gave the .480 to San Cristobal, who pointed it in the general direction of the proceedings as his minion forced Paula to lay backwards onto the platform and used the built-in restraints to secure her hands. He then unzipped her jacket all the way, letting it fall open and reveal her naked upper body. She began kicking him, but he was able to stop both of her legs with his big hands, after which he swiftly and expertly pulled off her pants, leaving her clad only in panties, and similarly secured her ankles under her. He threw her pants with a loud slap on the floor at San Cristobal's feet. What I could only describe as a low moan, long and weak, a moan of extreme despair, issued from somewhere deep within her, and continued as the Colombian took his gun from San Cristobal, took the bag, and, not saying a word, but with that silly evil grin still on his face, left us.

Paula continued her moaning as San Cristobal addressed me from his position on the other side of the device. "I can see from the expression on your face that you have met my woman," he said. I did not reply, but looked at the anguish on her face and then at the self-satisfied, almost placid smile on his. "You think not, eh?" At this, Paula moaned louder. I could see her leg muscles working. "She has been mine since she was a little girl of perhaps eleven or twelve. Of course, I was much younger then myself."

"You piece of shit!" she yelled suddenly, and then continued the moaning in an almost deranged way. It worried me that she could have been drugged or incapacitated in some other way. On the other hand, she had expressed her opinion of the topic quite succinctly.

San Cristobal continued, "Of course, Senór Komensky, I believe you are also quite familiar with another piece of property I have claimed as my own. You have fornicated with this one's sister, yes? Was she as good as when she was a little girl?"

"You are a piece of shit," I said calmly. "And you have a lot of nerve accusing me of fornication. You are a liar and a murderer masquerading as a man of God."

"True. I am all those things and much more, Senór Komensky."

I could see my cell phone next to the syringe on the top of the chest of drawers, but I couldn't see if the voice recorder was still going. "You had Linda killed!" I accused, hoping to get more of a confession from him. If old evidence couldn't be found, I'd settle for new.

"But," he said, raising a finger and shaking it in the air in front of his face. "Of the murders which have been committed here, I am guilty only of that of the lovely tattooed Senórita Cambrero." He turned suddenly and started rummaging in the chest of drawers with his back to the rest of us.

I tested the zip ties on my wrists and prepared to try to snap them if I could, while the monster kept talking. "My wife Linda San Cristobal seemed to have been unfortunately killed by a quirk of fate." Then he turned to face me again. "But you, Senór, have been duped by the same religious fanatics who would throw me from my church and deny the true god-given nature of the human race. Hypocrites!" A snarl curled his upper lip and rage filled his features. "Those pious Templars let that woman have their high-tech killing machines, and like all women she proved to be a weak, miserable failure. She couldn't even whore her way to success!"

"You must have hated your mother," I said, and then grinned at him. "You're a truly sick bastard. And your 'natural man' bullshit is what the church calls sin."

Partly, I think, in response to this, and partly to control the rage that seemed bound to burst out of his forehead at any moment, he turned and started going through the drawers again, as if looking for something, throwing sex toys this way and that. He spoke with his back turned. "So it doesn't bother you that Brother Morgan lied to you?"

I paused before answering. I still had a gun to my head, and my headache rivaled a full-on vice grip on my skull. I needed to calm down. Nothing wrong, I thought, with buying a little time. Sooner or later he'd make a mistake, and if it was later, I wanted to still be around to take advantage of it. With no immediate changes, other than Paula had stopped moaning, I asked, "Are you saying that the Templars—the Montesans I think they're called now—killed Dr. Cajo?"

Now facing me and ridiculously holding an orange plastic penis, San Cristobal said, "Oh, no! By that time, she had given up on finding the evidence being held by Cajo, that ingrate, that hypocrite, who would cut off the teat that suckled him."

"Then she worked for you!"

"If I were to tell you that the archdiocese paid her, you would not believe me. But you are a detective. I'm sure there is what you call a paper trail, if you look for it." He casually tossed the penis across the room as if it were a child's toy. It bounced and skipped through the railing and into the stairwell behind me. "But yes. Ultimately, I directed the people who approached her and proposed that Cajo giving the evidence he supposedly had against me to a Vatican organization would ultimately crumble the authority of the archdiocese and ruin the church. It wasn't a hard sell."

"That implies that you are going to give me a chance to look for it."

He looked first at his minion and then directly into my eyes. "Perhaps I will. But then I will have to exact some price for not only allowing you to live, but to repay me for allowing you to defile the beautiful Linda." He threw up his hands and then slapped them down hard on his thighs—a gesture of frustration. "What kind of a place is this? I do not find anything adequate in here. I will have to complain to the management." He kept looking this way and that, and then back at Burly, as if the guy holding the gun on me could pull what San Cristobal wanted out of thin air.

I took the opportunity to make an appeal. "Let us go. We have no evidence against you. Leave the country and go on your way. We can't hurt you."

"But you have." He walked closer to me now. I hoped to get a leg up into his groin, but he stopped short. "It was painfully obvious that you also failed to find the evidence that that *gordo*, Cajo hid so well. I am confident it either does not exist or it is lost for eternity, like my immortal soul. Don't look so shocked. If damnation is where I am headed, then we are all headed there together. One big happy fucking family!"

He put out his hand to the guy behind me and addressed him. "Juanello! Mi puñal!" Out of the corner of my eye, I could see that Burly had handed San Cristobal a Spanish dagger with an eight-inch double-sided blade, a brass guard and rosewood handle. There were some kind of fancy engravings on the polished steel of the blade. Hints of corrosion suggested a weapon of extreme age. I recognized the other stains on the blade as blood. Paula squirmed mightily against her bonds, and I tried to reassure her by looking first at her, then the blade, and then back again, shaking my head slightly as I did so. I was rewarded with the side of the barrel of my gun coming hard against the side of my head.

The monster wanted to torture us both with this threat of being stabbed to death. I thought it best not to say anything to anger him, but prepared to put myself and the chair in between San Cristobal and Paula if necessary, gun to the head or not. But San Cristobal walked back around to Paula's other side to face me, as if he were staging it for a camera. He stood over her face, looking into her eyes and displaying the dagger between them. His rapturous smile showed how much he was getting turned on by this process.

Finally, he said, addressing us both, "This is my favorite toy." He caressed the knife as if it were a lover. "You can keep your buzzing Japanese dildos and your little miniature balls. When I slide this into a woman, the ecstasy will be unbearable. As it was when I penetrated Senórita Cambrero's chest and drove my implement straight into her beating heart!"

"Stop!" I yelled. I couldn't have helped myself if I tried.

He placed the blade under Paula's chin, held it in position to cut her throat for just a second, and then removed it and fingered the very tip of the blade. "You don't want me to stop, Senór Komensky. You will be my witness. To pay for your violations, you will witness my ultimate consummation with this wife, this concubine, which I have claimed since before she was ready to bleed!" The last word came out like the snarl of some feral animal.

Paula then started to panic, looking this way and that and trying to see what Black Bishop San Cristobal's next move might be so that she could pull herself away from it. I knew I would have to make my move soon, though San Cristobal's kind of evil, in my experience, liked to deliver its reprisals on longer time scales. If taking action resulted in a bullet to my head, then, at least, I would have died trying. I just needed Paula to hold on a little bit longer; wait for that opening, wait to take advantage of all of the features of the device to which she'd been strapped. I knew she'd seen the same device in use at Beth's party, or at least I was only a percentage point short of knowing.

San Cristobal, enjoying the reaction to his threat, fondled the dagger for a few more seconds, then made a move that even I didn't expect. In a single, deft flourish, he sliced away the waistband of Paula's panties, just below her navel, and with his free hand tore them completely open at the front. Paula, in reaction to this, threw her head back and screamed. I don't know if it was the reaction she knew he wanted, or if she had really given up, if she really didn't have the faintest idea that all she would have to do is depress the sides of the device back with her thighs and it would fall apart like a tent of toothpicks and release her, the safety for those who only play at sexual torture. But I counted on the fact that San Cristobal's only experience with torture was in using real racks and real forceps of hot coals.

Whether or not Paula knew I counted on this, her reaction did, in fact, please San Cristobal. It pleased him as if he could die right there in a state of supreme euphoria with her scream echoing through his head for all eternity. I knew we were close to making a final move when he put his hand down his pants. "Get ready," I told myself.

The bastard slowly brought the dagger into position between Paula's legs. She squirmed but didn't scream again, and this seemed to disturb him. It interrupted the dagger's slow progress. I heard the faint sound of the latch releasing as she tightened her thighs against the platform.

The timing couldn't have been better if we had practiced it a hundred times. A bullet fired from outside blew through the blackout curtain on the front window and hit San Cristobal's knife hand with a whine followed by the sound of shattering bone. The dagger flew back and behind San Cristobal, but I could see it by looking between his legs. At the same moment, his minion reacted by taking my gun off me and leveling it at the invisible threat outside the window. San Cristobal, in a state of shock, staggered backward toward the back door with blood pouring from a neat hole in his right hand.

I could only imagine that the shot had been taken— somehow—by Georgio, but I didn't have time to ponder. With every ounce of strength I grasped the chair, and, with my hands still tied behind me, I pushed up and back with all my strength to drive the back of the chair under Burly's rib cage. It did the trick. He stumbled back, trying to catch his balance. A slug from my .38 slammed into the ceiling—it would have to alert others in the Tally house—so to keep him from aiming it again, I took a step backwards and pushed harder. Flailing and unsuccessfully trying to get a hold on the railing, the big oaf went over backwards into the stairwell. A man with less bulk may have survived the fall, but put two hundred ten pounds at a bad angle against a cervical vertebra and you get a pop that says broken neck without benefit of an expensive diagnosis.

It's funny how you train for struggles like that one, hours and hours of police training, training at the gym, sparring, maybe participating in amateur matches, join a dojo; when the chips—or whatever you use to signify that you are betting your life—are down, you never see the training or the face of your trainer, or even the faces of your loved ones. What you see is what is going to happen to you if you don't mix every ounce of that training with some kind of animal survival instinct, and then let it go. Sure you have to maintain the heroic stance, the difference between good and evil, but imminent death makes that line move around a lot, and awfully hard to see.

Pushing off from the stairwell railing, I threw a running block against San Cristobal's knees, throwing him off balance toward the back. Sliding on the hardwood, I rolled onto my back and grabbed the dagger blade as I slid over it. It sliced into my palm, causing a wave of burning pain, but I was able to juggle the handle enough to push twice and sever the zip tie. With my hands free, I found myself standing just in time to deflect a punch from San Cristobal's remaining good left hand and to throw a good left upper into his solar plexus, spreading my blood onto his black priest shirt. He doubled over, but we both saw the loose dagger on the floor at the same time and went for it. Unfortunately, he got it first, and I shrank back next to Paula. While she searched for her pants, I searched for something to use to defend myself in the upcoming knife fight.

Again, San Cristobal, snorting like an enraged bull, left us no time to engineer a margin of safety. Paula found her leather pants, but tossed them to me just in time for me to flick them at his thrust. The leather caught the blade of the dagger and looped onto the guard, allowing me to pull it out of his hands, take it in mine, and throw the pants back to Paula. I wasn't watching, but I'm guessing she put them on while I took a few swipes at his face. Then I went down low, slicing a deep gash into his left thigh that made him trumpet like a wounded rhino.

I gave it a few seconds to catch my breath and to watch him go down on that wounded leg, but he didn't. Instead, ignoring my menacing waves of the dagger, he went straight for Paula's throat. Before she or I could react, he had both hands, even the one with the bloody hole, around her neck. He towered over her, and she seemed helpless. Her face turned deep red and she pounded on his arms and tried to pry his hands off her as he shoved her to the front of the room next to the blackout curtain.

Intending to go after him and put the dagger through his back and into whatever he used as a beating heart, I took hold of it with both hands, and with the point aimed where I thought the best place between two ribs would be. But I didn't have to take another step. Another bullet chuffed through the drape and met its mark at San Cristobal's right temple, taking out a cone of tissue and blood from his head the size of an ice cream drumstick, and spattering it halfway to the back of the room. Even the devil in him couldn't make his hands hold the grip on Paula's neck any longer. She threw him off like a rag doll, and I heard the mangled mess of his head hitting the floor, making a sound like a dog food sliding out of the can and into the bowl.

"Drop it!" I heard the command from the officer in tac gear who had just burst through the back door, but I couldn't respond. The dagger had already fallen from my hands. All Paula and I could do was embrace each other and hope that the worst was over. For both of us.

CHAPTER NINETEEN

They told me to call this chapter "epilogue," but I looked it up and it didn't seem appropriate. Maybe "adaptation" would be better; or throwing in the proverbial towel. I don't know. I may have to adapt in a lot of ways.

Ops, my contract hacker, had certainly come through for me. Who would have guessed that not only would he be able to use the codes from Cajo's safe to access, download and distribute the evidence from the cloud to all interested parties, including an unforgiving Venezuelan government that saw the only way to prevent an out-and-out coup d'état was by vigorously pursuing the prosecution of every identifiable follower of the Black Bishop, but also could he gain operational control of all of the Montesan weapons. These included the UAV he used to get a high-resolution infrared image from inside Tally's third floor and to fire the .50 caliber rounds that took the bishop down with the accuracy of a trained sniper.

The darknet lost track of Ops within a week after he cashed my check, which I'd made out to cash and mailed to a blind box in Hyde Park. I know he'll surface again when the time is right, and I'm sure he's adapting.

The only player in San Cristobal's drama who managed to stay alive, Eddie Figg sang like a reality show runner-up. So the way I piece this together after all the time that went by and all the people who died is this:

The night that Dr. Cajo met his maker, he had gotten a call from Master and Commander Morgan. The call went something like: Your life and the evidence are both in danger because we couldn't keep the zipper up on our drone warehouse. We'd rather have the evidence even if you have to get it to us at the risk of your own life.

That's about when Figg saw the good doctor standing outside the museum pondering his mortality and enjoying the good April breeze off Lake Michigan.

Danita Cambrero, alias Danielle Silva Ensenada, already employed Figg for the sole purpose of getting her hands on the evidence. Whether she was working for the local archdiocese, for San Cristobal, or for both, Figg didn't know, and San Cristobal's rantings couldn't be trusted. Personally, based on her obvious distaste for authority, I think she was working for more than one side.

Cajo clearly had had misgivings, possibly instilled by the devious Ms. Cambrero, about turning the evidence over to the Montesans or holding it in paper form. By the night of his death, he had already digitized everything, uploaded it to the cloud, and secured it using passwords provided to him by his trusted assistant—you guessed it—Cambrero. It may come as no surprise that she already knew the passwords that would give her access and control of the Montesan flying circus. After all, she had them tattooed on her body. And it must have given her a good laugh at the stupid Dr. Cajo when she gave them to him to protect the most valuable thing he would ever do with his life.

That she had these codes also suggests she did, in fact, work for San Cristobal. But there's more. I think she was doubling as a Montesan operative, and tried to get control and stop the assault on Cajo's museum suite. She had to be supremely frustrated when she learned that Cajo had added a final password, a code she needed to get the evidence, a code she didn't have. She must have thought the additional code, the code that Cajo should have been too stupid to devise, was written down and still contained in that damn safe.

Back to Cajo's fate: Eddie followed Cajo up to the suite, drew his gun and hoped to force Cajo to give up the passcode at gunpoint. Cajo knew that, if a drone rocket destroyed the safe, nobody would have the code, and, as the bishop had speculated, the evidence would be lost in cyberspace. As Cajo was hurriedly writing it down on a piece of paper, Laxalt Johnson, the janitor, came unexpectedly walking through from the back office. Seeing this as an opportunity to get the code to the "trusted" Cambrero, he gave it and his firearm to Johnson, telling him to get it to Cambrero at any cost.

Johnson was on his way when he encountered Figg, who ordered him to turn over the paper he was holding, then shot him when he resisted. About then, the rocket hit the suite and Figg panicked, failed to hold onto the small piece of paper, and lost it somewhere in the smoke and chaos of the partially collapsed upper floor.

I know that an informant in DHS, probably a local follower of San Cristobal's twisted church, let somebody know I left a message for Doug Christie about evidence. I can't prove it, but I think Danita Cambrero was operating the drones that attacked me and Beth Pea. If she thought it would be better to have the passcode die with me than have me turn it over to DHS, she didn't count on San Cristobal showing up in Chicago looking for someone to blame, or on him ventilating her diaphragm with his Venezuelan pig sticker.

After the case resolved, I spent weeks agonizing over why San Cristobal chose to frame Linda for Cajo's murder, and the only thing I come up with is that he never let the sisters go. Like a cat toying with a captured mouse, he allowed them both to go on with their lives, even allowed Paula to marry the man whose son would help Cajo get the evidence out of Venezuela, but he never let them out of his sphere of influence, and—to mix metaphors, that's a word I learned writing this—he cast a wide net.

Figg will be prosecuted, of course. So will an unfortunately large number of priests and nuns who were exposed by the evidence, and particularly by San Cristobal's meticulous, obsessive lists. The control freak just couldn't help himself.

Beth Pea, despite her questionable judgment in letting her addiction spill over into her fund-raising duties at the museum, appears to have been criminally innocent though morally bankrupt. Yet she's a nut—actually a pea—that I can't crack. Maybe it's my weakened state, maybe the loss of my one true love, but every day brings me more and more trouble staying away from her.

The Catholic Church will survive, though not necessarily by the most moral of means. Since the revelations from the cloud, people are lining up to bear witness against those who exploited them in the name of an organization that was supposed to minister to windows and orphans. Politically, there will be an all-out, Vatican effort to minimize the damage. I haven't been able to get hold of Morgan, or any Montesan Templars, for that matter. My testimony about them will be barely believed when the media gets through spinning the facts, so I plan to keep any further statements short and sweet—as in: What Templars? Whether they or any other so-called catholic militia will be employed to silence witnesses remains to be seen. It could be a bloody, holy war.

These days, I find wars not worth the effort, and the world morally bi-directional. For me, any world that allowed the rape and torture of the two young Langhoeffer sisters, and the death of one of them, without any reasonable form of justice doesn't seem to measure up. That kind of injustice used to be my call to arms, a signal to ride to the rescue and a mandate to defenestrate the evil-doers. For a long time after this case, and without my Linda, I didn't know if I could pull that off. Now I don't know if I can. When Charlie Komensky falls, he apparently doesn't know how to find the soft landing spots.

When my blood pressure spiked right after our rescue, and when I told the medical tech that I was having trouble focusing my right eye, Georgio insisted that I forget about veterinarians and go to a real hospital. That resulted in the diagnosis I'm coping with as this manuscript is concluded. As Georgio correctly guessed, my head is hard as a rock, and a few blunt traumas aren't going to change that. I suppose I should be thankful that the tumor up there is benign, but it's growing ever so slowly and pushing against a blood supply. I might have to learn to aim with my left eye, as long as I stay conscious. Whether the state will let me keep my PI license remains to be seen.

I got a letter from Paula the other day. Her son had been held and tortured by San Cristobal's gang, but was released, and became a key witness in the Venezuelan prosecutions. She seemed happy, but confessed that she's as thoroughly haunted by what happened to Linda as am I.

This last part is going to sound like I made it up. I'm having trouble believing it myself, and I debated with myself about the wisdom of mentioning it here. In fact, I held onto this for a month after getting it, just to prove to myself that it wasn't a delusion brought on by the tumor. Whether I act on it depends on whether I decide that I can withstand another major disappointment, whether my condition gets any worse, and whether I can resist starting a relationship with Beth Pea, and everything that entails.

Eventually, I'll have it analyzed. It may turn out to be something else—an attempted con, a joke, an extortion, a way for some old enemy to get me out into the open and exact revenge, maybe worse. It could be some kind of sick message from the darknet—or from the Montesans.

But here goes. After I wrote the part about Paula's letter, the mailman delivered another one, postmarked from a small town in the middle of Nebraska. The text was computer printed on plain white paper, and the envelope had no return address. It says only this:

DEAREST CHARLIE:
I AM TRULY SORRY. A TRAIN RUNS NEAR HERE. IF YOU CAN EVER FORGIVE ME, WHEN YOU ARE UP TO IT, COME AND FIND ME. WITNESS PROTECTION SUCKS. THEY WILL MAKE IT VERY DIFFICULT.

L